VIRTUALLY IN LOVE

fLiRT

Read the entire Flirt series!

Lessons in Love

Never Too Late

Portrait of Us

Sunset Ranch

Puppy Love

Love Is in the Air

Sparks in Scotland

Our Song

VIRTUALLY IN LOVE

By A. Destiny and Catherine Hapka

SIMON PULSE

NEW YORK LONDON TORONTO SYDNEY NEW DELHI

This book is a work of fiction. Any references to historical events, real people, or real places are used fictitiously. Other names, characters, places, and events are products of the author's imagination, and any resemblance to actual events or places or persons, living or dead, is entirely coincidental.

SIMON PULSE
An imprint of Simon & Schuster Children's Publishing Division
1230 Avenue of the Americas, New York, New York 10020
First Simon Pulse paperback edition December 2015

Book designed by Regina Flath
The text of this book was set in Adobe Caslon Pro.
Manufactured in the United States of America
10 9 8 7 6 5 4 3 2 1
Library of Congress Control Number 2015953054
ISBN 978-1-4814-2118-8 (pbk)
ISBN 978-1-4814-2120-1 (eBook)

Chapter One

"Aesop's, anyone?"

I glanced up at Kazuo Aratani's grinning face, which had just popped into view over the top edge of my music stand. As usual, his black hair was sticking up in random tufts, making him look like a Muppet with better cheekbones.

"Sure," I said, already salivating at the thought of the amazingly greasy fries at our favorite diner. "We've got time before the S&D meeting. But give us a chance to put our instruments away first, okay?"

My other best friend, Vanessa Bennett, giggled from her seat across the way. "Seriously, Kaz," she said. "Did you even take your trumpet apart, or did you just shove it into your backpack?"

I grinned as Kaz stuck out his tongue at her. Everyone says

I'm pretty peppy, but when it comes to excess energy, I've got nothing on Kaz, the world's most hyper tenth grader. At least that's what our science teacher, Ms. Farley, always calls him.

Me? The teachers just call me Chloe Bell, Spaz Girl. Okay, kidding. Only a few of them actually call me that. The rest are probably thinking it, though. You crash into one little tower of donated food cans in the school lobby freshman year, and you're branded forever. For a while Vanessa called me the Tiny Tornado, but thankfully, that one didn't stick.

In any case, I figured the ten seconds or so since rehearsal had ended was plenty of time for Kaz to break down and put away his trumpet. And check his e-mail. And possibly cure cancer. You just never knew with Kaz.

"Okay, I'm ready. Let's eat," Vanessa said. "We'll need extra energy to deal with the S&D kids, right?" She snapped her flute case shut, then stood up so fast, she almost knocked over her music stand. Kaz caught it just in time.

But not before our band director, Mr. Graves, noticed the commotion. He glanced at Van over the tops of his wire-rimmed glasses. Or, rather, his spectacles—that's what Vanessa calls them, since they're so old-fashioned and proper looking, just like Mr. Graves himself.

"Everything under control, Ms. Bennett?" Mr. Graves asked in his dry, dusty voice. He might be a pretty good music teacher—and a freakishly great tuba player for such a skinny guy—but he looks and acts more like a librarian from an old movie.

"Fine, yeah," Vanessa said, blushing bright pink. Van is an open book. Every emotion she feels is painted right there on her pale cheeks and reflected in her big blue eyes. She's also crazy shy—always has been. I don't get that. She's smart and sweet and artsy and talented, not to mention beautiful—tall and willowy, with wavy blond hair that always behaves itself, unlike my own unruly mop of brown curls. But no matter how many times I point out her perfection, she just waves her hand and changes the subject.

Mr. Graves swept his cool grayish-blue eyes over the three of us. We smiled innocently back at him. Finally he turned away with a soft *harrumph*, returning to shuffling through his stack of sheet music.

"Okay, hurry up." Kaz started dancing from one foot to the other, his battered canvas shoes squeaking on the linoleum. "I'm starving to death."

"Yeah, right." I carefully tucked my mouthpiece into its velvet slot in my clarinet case. Spaz or not, I'm always careful with my instrument. "Mr. Graves might not have seen you scarfing those Cheez Doodles during the movie medley, but I did."

"Seriously." Vanessa glanced up and down Kaz's lean form. "I don't know how you eat so much and stay so skinny, Kaz."

"Look who's talking, skinny girl," Kaz shot back with a laugh.

I didn't hear whatever Van said next, because just then my cell phone vibrated in my pocket. I'd turned the sound off during band practice, which meant no hints from the ringtone—I have a different one programmed for just about everyone I know.

When I pulled out my phone, I smiled at the name on the screen. "Hang on," I told my friends. "I just got a text from Trevor."

"Uh-oh, it's Chloe's almost-boyfriend." Vanessa rolled her eyes dramatically. "Hope you're not really starving to death, Kaz. Because this might take a while."

"I still don't think this Trevor dude is even real," Kaz commented. "I mean, we've never seen him in person, right? Maybe it's like one of those romantic-comedy movie situations where she's trying to act all cool by sending lovey-dovey texts to herself from some alleged out-of-state dream guy, or . . ."

I didn't hear the rest. My attention was on the tiny screen of my phone.

Hey, Chloe, what's up?

Okay, it wasn't exactly a Shakespearean sonnet. But that was okay with me. Trevor and I were way past the point of needing to impress each other with clever texts. My thumbs flew over the touch screen as I responded.

Hi! Just finished after-school band practice. How was your day?

Vanessa peered over my shoulder. "Just send a few kissy lips and heart emojis already and let's go, okay?"

"Hang on." I waved her away, my eyes trained on the phone as I waited for a response to pop up. Moments later it did.

Good. Just wanted to check in before rehearsal. Might be late since we need to figure out what to do about our drummer situation.

I nodded. Trevor is in a band—not a concert-and-marching high school band like mine, but a supercool indie rock band he started himself. It's called Of Note. Clever, right? There are five members—or at least there were until a couple of weeks ago, when the drummer's family moved back to Puerto Rico.

Cool, I typed back. *Have fun, and text me later!*

Def. Bc I might have something big to tell u. More later maybe.

What do u mean? Something big like what?

LOL, be patient, impatient girl! Don't want to tell u until I'm sure it's happening. Gtg. Catch u later.

I sighed with frustration and smiled at the same time. Trevor knew me so well! He was probably cracking himself up, knowing I was already going crazy wondering what his big news might be. Meanwhile, he was probably just going to tell me he'd bought some new guitar strings or something.

Then again maybe not. He'd said he wanted to wait until he was sure it was happening. Could there really be any doubt about new guitar strings? Maybe he really did have big news. But what? My thumbs hovered over the keypad, tempted to demand more right then and there.

But I knew better. I'm pretty good at wheedling what I want out of people, but Trevor is no pushover. Besides, he always turns his phone off when the band is rehearsing. Which meant I could send him the most charming and persuasive text in the world, and he still wouldn't see it until later. I'd just have to wait and wonder.

Okay, have a great practice, I typed, then turned off my phone and tucked it away.

Only then did I look up at my friends. Most of the other band members had left by then, and Mr. Graves was carefully sliding some papers into his battered briefcase as he prepared to leave too. Kaz was tapping his foot and watching me. Vanessa was scrolling through messages on her own phone.

"So, what's up with Mr. Wonderful today?" Kaz asked. "Did the Rolling Stones beg him to join yet?"

"Get real. Like he'd really want to jam with those old geezers." I smirked, knowing that would bug Kaz. He loves classic rock—the older and moldier, the better. Then again he also loves bluegrass, Gilbert and Sullivan operettas, and hardcore punk. That's Kaz for you. He's interested in everything, even stuff nobody else cares about. It's one of my favorite things about him, even if it means I have to put up with his creaky old music sometimes.

Vanessa looked up from her phone. "Oh good, you're finally done. Can we go already?"

So we did. I quickly finished packing up my clarinet, and soon the three of us were in the quiet hallway, which as usual smelled like a combination of bleach and dirty sweat socks. Just one of the joys of a school where the gym and the music wing are right next to each other.

Kaz was whistling as he walked, juggling two instrument cases along with his overstuffed backpack. He plays three instruments in the band—trumpet, oboe, and clarinet. But there are plenty of other good clarinet players, including yours truly, so he doesn't even bring his clarinet with him much anymore. He'd started out as first chair clarinet in the elementary school orchestra, and I'd been second chair. But we'd goofed around so much that the music teacher ended up separating us by introducing Kaz to the oboe. It's similar to the clarinet but much harder to play, so she probably figured it would keep him busy enough to stay out of trouble. Little did she expect him to master it in about a week and a half—okay, I'm exaggerating, but only a little!—and start using it to make fart sounds during the slow parts of songs.

Anyway, in fourth grade Kaz went through a brief phase where he got all self-conscious about hanging out mostly with girls—that would be me and Vanessa, who'd joined our little nerd clique when her family moved to town in second grade—and took up the trumpet. He'd been switching around ever since.

"So, what did Trevor want?" Vanessa asked.

"He was just checking in." Thinking about Trevor made me smile, as always. "He's off to rehearse with his band."

Kaz stopped whistling. "Let me guess. They're going to perform variations on that lame pop song you like so much."

"You mean the *totally awesome* song 'True Romance' by the Sly Guys?" I said. "Possibly. Of Note already covers it, and their version is even more amazing than the original."

Vanessa giggled as Kaz let out a snort. "Come on, Kaz," she said. "You have to admit, it's a pretty catchy song."

"I suppose it's okay musically, if a bit derivative." Kaz swung his oboe case back and forth. "But the lyrics? Lame and full of clichés."

"If you say so." I checked my watch. "Come on. Let's hurry. We don't have that much time before the meeting."

Aesop's Diner doesn't look like much from the outside. Actually, it doesn't look like much from the inside, either. The floor is dingy, the seats battered, and the lighting bad. But the place has the most extensive menu I've ever seen, and almost everything on it is good.

"Who wants to go first?" Kaz asked as he slid into our favorite booth, sitting across from me and Vanessa.

I reached for the stack of menus the waitress had dropped on the table before she'd hurried off. "Me!" I sang out. "Here goes . . ."

The menu is enormous, like I said, but whoever designed it apparently didn't believe in wasting paper. So the print is tiny, cramming hundreds of choices onto just two large, laminated pages. Kaz opened one of the menus flat in front of me and then started slowly spinning it around on the table. Closing my eyes, I waited a moment. Then I stabbed downward with my finger.

When I opened my eyes, Vanessa was leaning forward to see where my finger had landed. "Lemon meringue pie," she read.

Kaz looked pleased. "Great, I'm in the mood for a serious sugar rush right now."

"Me too," Vanessa said. "My turn next?"

"Go for it." Pulling my finger away, I took over spinning duty from Kaz. That's an important part of our game—we've been to Aesop's so often that we all pretty much have the menu memorized. The spinning keeps us from cheating by aiming in the general direction of the food we want.

Vanessa's finger came down on a line near the bottom corner. "Ugh," I said. "Decaf coffee."

"Nice going, genius." Kaz rolled his eyes. "Let me at it. I'll get us some real food."

"Be my guest." Vanessa pushed the menu toward him.

As I started spinning it again, Kaz flexed his fingers and cracked his knuckles, making a big show of getting ready. Finally he closed his eyes.

"Round and round she goes," I intoned.

"Where she stops, nobody knows," Kaz finished, jamming his finger down on the last word.

I leaned forward, grabbing his finger to move it aside. "Mushroom and cheese omelet," I read. "Gross. I hate mushrooms."

"Want to pick one more, then?" Vanessa offered.

I nodded. That was part of the game. We had to order everything we chose at random, but if we wanted to, we could pick more than three things. This time my finger landed on onion rings, and I smiled.

"That's more like it," I said, looking around for the waitress.

After we'd ordered, I shot a wadded-up straw wrapper at Kaz. "So listen," I said. "Birthday boy, we need to figure out what to do for your party."

"Definitely!" Vanessa's eyes widened. "I can't believe it's coming up so soon."

"I know, right?" Kaz leaned back in his seat and sighed. "I'm already feeling so much older and wiser than you two."

I laughed. "Older, maybe. Wiser? I think not."

"Ah, the arrogance of youth," Kaz said in a mock-serious tone, shaking his head.

I rolled my eyes. Kaz is exactly two months older than I am, which means we'd been going through variations of this same exchange forever. Or at least before we could walk, because Kaz and I have been friends since we were in diapers—literally. I inherited my energy from my mother, who can't sit still for more than two seconds at a time. So when I was born, it took Mom about a week to get bored sitting around on maternity leave, taking care of one baby. She was used to running a whole company, so I guess changing my diapers and feeding me strained peas or whatever wasn't that much of a challenge. Anyway, she decided to bring in a little extra money by starting an in-home day care, and Kaz was one of her first customers. His mother died when he was, like, six months old, and his dad works long hours as an orthodontist with his own practice.

Actually, Kaz's dad is so busy that he tends to forget little details, like his son's birthdays. So there was definitely no surprise Sweet Sixteen bash in the works at that end. Which stunk, since if anyone deserved a big blowout party, it was Kaz.

Then again what are best friends for? I figured Van and I

could come up with something fun, even if it didn't look much like the fancy Sweet Sixteen parties on TV.

Vanessa seemed to be thinking along the same lines. "So, how are we going to celebrate such a momentous occasion?" she mused.

"It needs to be big." I drummed my fingers on the table. "I mean, now that he's so old and all, who knows how long poor old Kaz has left to party?"

He snorted with laughter. "Right. They might not allow parties at the old folks' home."

"Maybe we should have a movie party," Vanessa suggested. "Play all Kaz's favorite monster movies or whatever."

"We did that two years ago," I reminded her. "I can't sit through *Creature from the Black Lagoon* yet again. Besides, turning sixteen is a big deal. We have to do something special."

"Are you saying *Creature from the Black Lagoon* isn't special?" Kaz protested.

Any response was interrupted by the waitress, rushing over with our coffee and onion rings. "Resta yer order'll be out in a sec," she mumbled, dropping the onion rings platter and extra plates in front of us and sloshing half the coffee out as she slammed down the mug.

"Thanks," Kaz called to her departing back.

Meanwhile, I grabbed the biggest onion ring in one hand and my phone in the other.

"What are you doing?" Vanessa asked, dabbing at the spilled coffee with a napkin.

I snapped a photo of myself chomping on the deep-fried goodness. Then I inhaled the rest of the ring, wiped my fingers on my napkin, and texted the picture to Trevor. "I like to give Trev a taste of my daily life," I explained as I hit send.

"Then you should send him a picture of you loading the dishwasher," Kaz suggested.

Vanessa giggled. "True. Or maybe one of you snoring in history class."

"You two are a laugh riot." I stuck my phone into my pocket. "But back to party planning."

Kaz helped himself to an onion ring. "Seriously, my birthday doesn't have to be a big deal," he said. "It'll be cool with me if Chloe just promises not to spend half of it texting Mr. Big-Time Rock Star."

As if on cue, my phone buzzed. Grabbing it out of my pocket, I smiled. "Speak of the devil," I said. "It's Trevor calling. Better take this—be right back."

I grabbed another onion ring and slid out of the booth, hitting the button to answer the call at the same time.

"Hi," I said as I hurried down the hallway leading to the restrooms, where I'd have a little privacy. "I thought you were practicing all afternoon?"

"I thought so too." Trevor has the best voice—soft and sweet but sort of gravelly and gruff, too. Totally rock star. "Zach forgot he had a dentist appointment, so we had to reschedule."

"Bummer."

"Sort of," he agreed. "At least there's a silver lining—now I get to talk to the cutest and most talented girl I know."

"That is a bonus," I agreed, trying not to let on how much his compliments always made me melt.

"Cute picture, by the way," he said. "Makes me wish I were there."

"Me too," I said with a smile. "Unfortunately, I can't talk long right now, though. My friends and I are just at the diner, fueling up for our S&D meeting—it starts in, like, ten minutes."

"S&D?"

"Song & Dance?" I prompted. "It's that volunteer group I've told you about."

"Oh yeah." He sounded a little uncertain. "Something about poor kids and music, right?"

"Uh-huh." Thinking about the group made me smile. "Our whole pep club volunteers with them—we're even doing a fund-raiser for them soon. Didn't I tell you about that?"

"Maybe," he replied. "Is that what your meeting's about?"

"No, this is just the regular monthly meeting." I leaned against the wall, twirling a stray curl around my finger. "Some people from the group's main office in the city gather up a bunch of kids and bring them out to our community center, and—"

"Oh right. And you guys teach them music. You did tell me about that. Sorry, guess I'm so distracted by this drummer thing, I can't keep anything else in my head." He gave a little self-deprecating laugh. "I remember now, though. It always sounded pretty cool."

"It is." I stepped to the end of the hallway, peering across the diner to see if my friends had polished off all the food yet. "Anyway, I should probably go, I guess. Sorry. Maybe we can talk later?"

"Sure. Have fun, Chloe. Later."

"Bye."

As I hung up, I suddenly remembered his mysterious text from earlier. What had that been about? He hadn't even mentioned it just now. For a second I was tempted to call back, but then I checked the time and realized it would have to wait. Hurrying to the booth, I slid back in next to Vanessa.

"How's Mr. Wonderful?" Kaz asked, grabbing the last onion ring off the plate.

"Hey!" I protested.

He grinned, leaned his head back, and opened his mouth, dangling the onion ring over it. Just before it touched his lips, he relented, tossing it over onto my plate.

I smiled and popped it into my own mouth before he could change his mind and take it back. "Thanks," I mumbled with my mouth full. "And since you asked, Trevor is great. I just asked him if his band can come play at your party, and he's totally on board."

Obviously, that was a joke, and they both knew it, since Trevor lives, like, three hours away. But while Vanessa laughed on cue, Kaz faked a look of horror. "No boy bands allowed!" he said, making a little X with his fingers as if warding off a vampire.

That made Vanessa laugh even harder. I just rolled my eyes.

"Hey, what can I say?" I cracked in return. "I figured live music would be the best way to get people to actually come to your party."

Kaz just grinned and grabbed the coffee from Vanessa to take a sip, not looking too worried. He might be a classic nerd in some ways, but Kaz is surprisingly popular at school. And everywhere else, come to think of it. Oh, things hadn't started out that way. Back in early elementary school, he got picked on by some of the bullies now and then. But he was such a nice guy that even the worst of the jerks seemed to feel kind of bad about it. It didn't hurt that his cousin Maya is a popular cheerleader who's a grade ahead of us. Or that I'm like a Chihuahua—always willing to bark in the face of a bigger, tougher dog, especially if that big dog starts messing with one of my friends.

"So, back to your birthday," I said after swallowing the onion ring. "What do you want for your gift this year?"

Kaz took a noisy slurp of the decaf and then pushed it over to Vanessa. "You guys don't have to get me anything."

I picked up a fork and helped myself to some pie, which the waitress had delivered while I was gone. "You say that every year. Can we drop the charade this time? You know Van and I are getting you something. So what do you want? A year's supply of oboe reeds? Tickets to that weirdo Gilbert and Sullivan group you like so much?"

"No, I'm serious. You don't need to buy me anything like that. Just the party is enough." Kaz reached across and picked a mushroom out of the omelet, which Vanessa was in the process of devouring. “Besides, you definitely shouldn’t spend any more money on me than you have to. We need to save up our spare cash so we can sponsor each other at the dance marathon. It’s only a couple of weeks away now, you know.”

He had a point. The fund-raiser I’d mentioned to Trevor was rapidly approaching. Song & Dance was such an incredible group that our pep club had voted unanimously to have a fund-raiser to support them. At first we’d been looking at doing something like a bake sale or maybe a concert, since most of the school band was in the pep club. But then Kaz had come up with something much more fun—a dance marathon. He got the idea from some old movie.

“Okay,” I said. “But if you don’t want us to spend money, what are you expecting? Homemade dandelion bracelets?”

“Nope. Just the pleasure of your company.” He grinned at both of us.

Vanessa and I traded a dubious look. “We’ll see,” she said, scooping up one last bite of egg. “But for now, we should get going. We don’t want to be late.”

Chapter Two

The community center was right across the street from Aesop's, so about five minutes later we were walking into the big auditorium where we always had our S&D meetings. There's a stage at one end with a piano on it. The rest of the room is one enormous open space. A whole bunch of folding chairs were stacked at one end; they use them for plays and other stuff, but we usually leave the place mostly clear so the kids can run around.

Kaz's cousin Maya was over in front of the stage, her perky, glossy black ponytail bouncing as she laughed at something one of band's trombonists was telling her. Most of the other cheerleaders and probably half the band were milling around nearby.

"Oh good." Vanessa's eyes scanned the place as we entered. "The kids aren't here yet, so we didn't miss anything."

I smiled at her. "Don't worry," I said. "They wouldn't dare start without you."

Kaz laughed, and Vanessa rolled her eyes at both of us. But it's true. She was the whole reason our school got involved with Song & Dance. She'd found the group's website last year and almost single-handedly convinced everyone in the pep club that we should hook up with them, even though the city where they're located is almost an hour's drive away.

That was Vanessa for you, though. She seems quiet and kind of passive sometimes, but she's tougher than any of us when it comes to stuff she cares about. And she definitely cares about kids. She adores them all, from the brattiest eight-year-old to the drooliest, smelliest baby. She's been babysitting since she was eleven, and she's planning to major in child psychology in college.

Maya spotted us and hurried over. "The bus driver just called and they're almost here," she said, smoothing down her already perfectly smooth hair. "She suggested we start with dance today since it rained yesterday and the kids are pretty hyper from being cooped up inside."

We all nodded obediently, which is the best thing to do when Maya is in charge.

"Can't wait to show them some moves," Kaz said, hopping around in what was probably supposed to be a tap dance of some sort.

The trombonist, who had followed Maya over, snorted loudly.

"Maybe we should leave the dancing to the cheerleaders, bro," he said, giving Kaz a slap on the back.

I grinned as the others—including Kaz—laughed. Kaz is famous for his goofy dance moves. When he was teaching everyone to do the Hustle at the homecoming dance last year, he accidentally stepped on the vice principal's foot and gave one of Maya's cheerleader friends an elbow to the jaw. Someone even shot a video, which went semiviral on the school website. One of the comments compared Kaz to a marionette on a sugar rush. Which had led to Vanessa and me calling him Pinocchio for a week or two.

A few minutes later a stout, smiling woman with wild gray hair and a whistle around her neck appeared in the doorway.

"There's Ms. Sokolofsky," Vanessa said.

The woman spotted us and waved. Then she turned and let out a shrill tweet on her whistle.

"In here, kiddoes!" she sang out.

The kids came pouring in. Song & Dance helps kids from all over the region who don't have access to good music education, whether because they're living in a women-and-children's shelter in the city or attending a poor rural school with no full-time music teacher—or whatever other reason. Sometimes kids come only once or twice until their families are back on their feet, while others have been coming for as long as we've been having our meetings.

"Hi, guys!" Vanessa called, lighting up like a candle as she beamed at all of them.

As she hurried off to help a pair of tiny girls who were in

danger of getting trampled by some of the bigger, more excitable boys, I spotted one of my favorite regulars, an undersize eight-year-old with an oversize attitude named Carlos. Today he was dragging a pale red-haired kid by the arm as he hurried in.

"Hey, C-man," I greeted him. "What's up?"

"The sky, duh!" Carlos retorted, wearing his usual saucy grin. Then he hooked a thumb in the other kid's direction. "This is Aidan. He's new."

"Hi, Aidan. I'm Chloe. Nice to meet you." I stuck out my hand. Aidan looked surprised; he peered at me suspiciously before tentatively shaking my hand.

Nearby, Kaz was tugging on one of the many braids of an adorable six-year-old regular named Shani. "Yo, who's up for some dancing?" he asked her, shuffling his feet in a weird little boogie move.

Shani and most of the other kids laughed, but Aidan just stared. Most people have that reaction the first time they see Kaz dance. I'm pretty sure Kaz dances to the beat of his own drummer, or whatever that expression is.

"So, Aidan, do you like dancing?" I asked brightly.

He just shrugged, staring at his own feet. I'd seen his type before—most of the kids who ended up with the group had gone through some pretty terrible stuff, and while some bounced back quickly, like Carlos, others were kind of shell-shocked for a while. It always made me sad, and being sad always makes me want to make things better.

But before I could figure out how to help Aidan, Maya jumped up onstage and clapped for attention. "Time to dance, kids!" she called out in her peppiest cheerleader voice. "Who's ready to have some fun?"

Some of the kids cheered. Others just stared at her. Carlos hooted loudly and did some cool break dancing moves.

Kaz laughed. "Hey, maybe Carlos should be today's demo dancer," he called out, high-fiving the kid and then doing a little breaking of his own. At least that was my best guess as to what he was doing as his long limbs flew randomly in every direction. I sneaked a peek at Aidan to see if he was laughing like everyone else, but he was still just staring solemnly at the floor. Yikes, this one was going to be tough.

Maya peered out at Kaz, clearly holding back a smile. "No break dancing today," she said sternly. "Since we're all psyched for the dance marathon, we're going to practice partner dancing today."

"Partner dancing?" an older kid I didn't recognize called out. "What's that?"

"I want to do line dancing again!" a cute little blond girl exclaimed.

A few other kids cheered, and I traded a smile with Kaz. Last month the cheerleaders had taught the kids some of their routines, and most of them had loved it.

But a few of the boys booed, including Carlos. "Let's just free-style, man!" he called out.

"Sorry, dude," Kaz told him. "You all want to be ready to raise tons of money for your new piano, right?"

Almost everyone cheered at that. I'd been to the Song & Dance headquarters once, and their ancient upright was on its last keys. The money from our fund-raiser was supposed to help buy them a new one, along with some other instruments and snacks and who knows what else for the kids.

"Kaz is right," Maya said when the cheers died down. "Part of how we're raising money is by charging people money to dance with us at the marathon. You all want to help, right?"

More cheers. Carlos started bragging loudly about how much money he was going to raise, and some of the other kids joined in. I smiled at Kaz, and he winked at me.

Finally Maya had to get Ms. Sokolofsky to whistle for attention.

"Okay," Maya said when most of the kids were sort-of listening. "Partner dancing it is, then."

"Aw, I was hoping we could do some clogging today," I called out with a grin, hoping to make Aidan smile. No dice.

"Just for that, you can be our demo dancer, Chloe." Maya smirked at me. "And your partner can be my dear cousin Kaz."

"What?" I put a hand to my heart, feigning horror. "But I *like* my toes!"

Carlos shouted with laughter. "Good one, Chloe!" he exclaimed, high-fiving me.

Meanwhile, Kaz stepped up to me and swept into a gallant bow. "Shall we, milady?" he said, holding out his hand.

"We shall." I dropped a brief curtsy and then took his hand. When he just stood there for a second, I decided to take the lead, twirling him around toward me, which made everyone laugh. Out of the corner of my eye, I noticed even Aidan had finally cracked a small smile. Score!

That made me ham it up even more. "Time for a dip, dippy," I announced.

Kaz knew exactly what to do. When I yanked him toward me, he let me dip him, collapsing into my arms afterward.

"Oof," I said. "You're heavier than you look!"

We wobbled, and a second later Kaz landed on his rear end at my feet. He clutched my legs, pulling himself up with exaggerated effort. That cracked the kids up even more, though Maya was rolling her eyes.

"Enough of the vaudeville act, you two," she said. "Maestro? Let's get started."

She pointed to one of the other cheerleaders, who was manning the sound system. A moment later classical music poured out of the speakers.

"Whoa, what is this?" Carlos exclaimed, wrinkling his nose.

"Music," Kaz informed him as he swept me into waltz position. "We'll be creating more of it later. But for now watch and learn, munchkins."

"Watch my toes get squashed," I added.

Shani giggled. "Be careful, Kaz!" she said. "Don't squash her toes!"

"I can't make any promises," he replied, straight-faced.

To my surprise, though, my toes were safe so far. "Hey, have you been practicing your waltzing?" I asked as we twirled around the room. "I don't have any broken bones yet or anything."

"I'm full of surprises." He smiled down at me and waggled his eyebrows.

I smiled back, a little distracted, as I suddenly noticed he was taller than the last time we'd danced together. When had that happened?

Meanwhile, Maya was talking to the kids, explaining what we were doing and using one of her friends to demonstrate the proper position. "Now, you guys, go ahead and try," she urged. "Grab a partner and waltz your little heinies off!"

She and the other volunteers made their way out onto the dance floor, offering to dance with any of the kids who seemed interested. Carlos made a beeline for a passing cheerleader, leaving Aidan stranded. Some of the other kids were already pairing up with one another.

I glanced around for Vanessa, knowing she'd be the perfect person to bring Aidan out of his shell, but I couldn't see her. Meanwhile, Shani was coming toward us. She poked me on the hip as we waltzed past.

"Hey, I want to cut in," she announced.

Kaz stopped short, clutching me to him so tightly, I couldn't breathe. "Oh no!" he exclaimed with exaggerated dismay. "You want to steal my partner, Chloe, away from me?"

Shani giggled and tugged on one of her braids. "No, silly!" she exclaimed. "I want to dance with *you*!"

"Oh!" A wide, goofy grin spread across his face, though he didn't loosen his grip much. "In that case, I guess it's all right. Just let me give her one last big hug, okay?"

"Okay," Shani agreed, though she sounded slightly impatient.

Kaz squeezed me even closer. I was a little breathless by then—lack of oxygen, I guess—and a little confused, too. What was he doing?

He lowered his face to my ear. "Check out Mr. Carrot Top over there," he whispered, his warm breath tickling my cheek. "Think he could use a partner."

Ah. I should have known Kaz would notice the lonely newbie too. "I'm on it," I whispered back, giving him a quick peck on the cheek—just to play it up a little more for Shani.

Kaz looked a bit startled by that as he quickly released me. "Okay, I'm all yours, Shani," he said, shooting me one last glance. "Let's dance."

I hid a smile as I hurried off. It takes a lot to surprise Kaz, and I was always pretty proud of myself when I managed it.

But there was no time to gloat just then. Aidan had backed up against the wall, and he looked pretty miserable.

I walked up to him. "Hi there, Aidan," I said cheerfully. "Will you dance with me?"

He shrugged, not meeting my eyes. "I dunno," he mumbled, his voice so soft, I could barely hear it. "I'm not a very good dancer."

"Oh, I bet you're better than you think." I leaned over and smiled at him. "You're probably better than I am. My dad used to say I had two left feet because I was always tripping up the stairs." That was true, though it was mostly because I was too impatient to walk up like a normal person and always insisted on taking the steps two or three at a time, even when I was way too young and short to manage it.

The boy's eyebrows shot up in surprise, and his mouth twitched as if he weren't quite sure whether I was joking. "Do you really want to dance with me?"

"I really do," I assured him. "Pretty please?"

I held out my hand, and after a long moment of hesitation, he took it. He didn't seem sure of what to do next, so I just shuffled my feet a little, not worrying too much about actual steps.

"So, one fun thing to do while we're dancing is to talk to each other," I told him. "What do you want to talk about?"

I was already coming up with a few possible topics, since I was guessing all I'd get was another "I dunno." To my surprise, though, he was ready with an answer.

"Is that guy your boyfriend?" he blurted out.

I blinked, not sure who he meant for a second. "Oh—you mean Kaz?" I suppose it was no surprise he thought so, given the way we'd been acting. "No, we're just friends. Best friends. We were just kidding around, pretending to be boyfriend and girlfriend."

"Oh." Aidan thought about that for a second. "Do you have a boyfriend?"

I shot another look at Kaz, who was goofing off nearby, doing some kind of modified tango with Shani. "As a matter of fact, I do," I told Aidan. "His name is Trevor."

"Oh." Now the kid looked nervous. "Will he be mad you're dancing with me?"

"No way," I assured him, twirling him carefully out of the way as Kaz and Shani boogied past. "He won't mind at all. You're doing him a big favor, actually."

"I am?"

"Yeah. See, Trevor lives really far away. Like, three hours drive at least."

"Huh?" Aidan exclaimed. "What are you talking about? How can he be your boyfriend if he's way far away like that?"

His voice was louder, and his eyes were bright and curious. Yay! Apparently, Vanessa wasn't the only one who could bring a shy kid out of his shell.

"Trevor and I met at music camp when we were just a little older than you," I told him. "We bonded over our love of music."

I smiled at the familiar memory. Back then Trevor had been a violinist. He was first chair in his school orchestra and had even gotten to play at the governor's mansion once. At camp they encouraged us to try out different instruments. At first Trevor hadn't been interested, but then one of the counselors offered to help him learn guitar. And the rest, as they say, is history.

"So he's been your boyfriend since you were my age?" Aidan asked in amazement, snapping me out of my reminiscing.

I twirled him around again. The kid was actually a pretty good dancer, even though he was more focused on what I was saying than what our feet were doing.

"No, definitely not that long," I said. "We stayed in touch for a little while after camp ended. Trevor's family lived only about half an hour away then, so we even got together a couple of times. But then his family moved out of state, and we lost touch."

"Oh." He looked confused. "But he's your boyfriend now?"

"Yeah, we found each other online a few months ago." Once again I couldn't help drifting into the familiar but still delicious memories of that day. "True Romance" had just hit number one on the charts, and I was on my favorite music message board talking about it when one of the other members—one I'd chatted with lots of times about other cool bands—said he was a guitarist whose band had done a cover of the song. He posted a video link, and when I played it, I recognized the guitarist immediately. It was Trevor! He was taller than the last time I'd seen him, of course, and much cuter, with floppy dark hair and contact lenses instead of the wire-rimmed glasses he used to wear. But the delicate fingers, his sharp little chin, those intense green eyes—I would have known him anywhere. As soon as he knew it was me, it was as if camp had ended five minutes ago instead of five years.

We'd been flirting nonstop ever since. At least I guess that's what it was. I didn't have much experience with flirting, given that I'd never even gone on a real date before. Not unless you count dressing up in tuxedos and ball gowns with Kaz and Vanessa for all the school dances and going as a threesome. Which I totally don't.

But I'm not shy, and I got the hang of the flirting thing quickly. Before long Trevor and I were texting daily and talking on the phone at least a couple of times per week. It wasn't long after that when my friends started calling him my almost-boyfriend and agreeing that the way we'd reconnected was the most romantic thing ever.

It had been a few months now, and things between us were hotter than ever. I mean, we were pretty much living out the lyrics to "True Romance"—at least the first verse, which starts with:

You meet cute, and the sparks fly.
You know you just met your dream girl or guy. . . .

Pretty much us, right?

Although when I thought about it, we'd never really talked about exactly what we had going. Friendship? Or true romance? I definitely knew which way *I* was leaning, and I was pretty sure Trevor felt the same way, but neither of us had ever brought it up. Which made me wonder: Was that what he wanted to tell me—what he was hinting at in that text? That he wanted us to be, you know, boyfriend-girlfriend? If only I'd thought to ask him when he'd called at the diner earlier . . .

"Ouch!" I blurted out as I felt someone poke me in the shoulder.

It was Vanessa. “Who’s your friend?” she asked, smiling at Aidan.

“I’m not telling you,” I said, clutching Aidan’s hands more tightly. “He’s all mine!”

That made the little boy giggle, which made my heart happy. He wasn’t turning out to be such a tough case after all.

“I’m Aidan,” he told Vanessa. “I like your hair—it’s pretty.”

“Why, thank you!” she said, touching her blond bangs. “I like your hair too. Will you dance with me?”

Aidan shot me a slightly worried look. “Um . . .”

“Go ahead,” I told him with a smile. “I need a drink of water anyway. But hey, maybe we can jam together later when we switch over to music, okay?”

“Sure.” He grinned at me and then turned back to Vanessa.

I winked at her over his head as they started to dance. Then I wandered off, looking for any other kids who might need a partner. As I passed Kaz, he broke away from Shani.

“Be right back, okay?” he told her. “I just want to talk to Chloe for a sec.”

He grabbed my arm and steered me to a corner of the room, away from the others. “Everything okay?” he asked when we were more or less alone.

“Sure.” I shrugged. “What do you mean? Why wouldn’t it be?”

“No reason.” He hesitated, cocking his head and looking at me kind of oddly. “It’s just, you—um, before. Why’d you kiss me like that?”

"Why not?" It wasn't as if I'd never kissed him before. We'd traded hand kisses and cheek kisses and even one hilarious elbow kiss for various silly photo ops. We'd even kissed on the lips once when we were around five, just to see what it was like. At the time, our conclusion had been that it was weird and kind of icky.

None of those kisses had been awkward at all. But suddenly this one was, at least after the fact.

"Okay," Kaz said, looking uncomfortable. "I just thought I'd ask, you know, in case you—"

The buzz of my cell phone interrupted him. It was Trevor's text tone.

Kaz recognized it too. "Mr. Wonderful," he murmured. "You'd better get that."

"Yeah." I wasn't so sure. What was going on here between me and Kaz? What had he been about to say? Still, I couldn't resist glancing down at the text.

U around later? Big news!!!

I felt a shiver of curiosity—was he finally going to spill that secret he'd mentioned? When I glanced up again, all I saw was Kaz's back as he danced away from me.

Oh well. Whatever was up with Kaz, I could figure it out later. I quickly texted Trevor back, then hurried over to join Vanessa, who was dancing with Aidan in a circle with three giggling little girls.

Chapter Three

"No phone at the table, Chloe," my mom said.

I glanced up sharply, my hand freezing halfway to my phone. I swear, the woman has ears like a bat. Or whatever animal can hear a pin drop from a mile away—or a phone vibrate on a daughter's lap at the dinner table.

My younger brother, Timothy, smirked at me through a mouthful of peas. "She can't help it, Mom," he said in his snottiest voice. "All teenagers are, like, addicted to their phones."

"Just wait," I told him. "Your turn's coming. Only a year to go until you're a teenager too."

"And we can't wait," my dad said dryly.

As my mom glanced at him with a chuckle, I sneaked a quick peek at the phone screen. It was Trevor, just as I'd expected.

"May I be excused, please?" I blurted out.

Dad raised an eyebrow. "What do you think?"

"I think that's a yes?" I said hopefully.

Mom shook her head. "You know the rules, Chloe." She reached for another helping of fish. "It's your turn to clear tonight. That means no phone or computer until the dishwasher is full and running."

"But, Mom—" I began.

"Enough, Chloe," she cut me off. "Whatever dire emergency is brewing in teenland, it will just have to wait."

I gritted my teeth, wanting to argue further but resisting the urge. I was dying to hear Trevor's voice. I mean, sure, I'd talked to him at the diner earlier. But that hardly counted.

It seemed like a million years later when the last plate was scraped and tucked into its slot in the dishwasher and I was finally able to escape to my room. As the door swung shut behind me, I was already calling Trevor.

"Hey, Chloe," he answered on the second ring. "What's up?"

I smiled and sank onto the bed. "Hey," I said. "Sorry I couldn't answer before—parents, dinner table, you know."

"Yeah." He sounded a little distracted. "But listen, huge news!"

"What?" I leaned back against the soft bulk of my favorite stuffed animal, Gordo the wonder pig, wondering if this was it—the moment Trevor would tell me I was the girl for him. Sort of like that line from "True Romance"—*When you know it's right, it's time to declare / Make it a memory you two will always share. . . .*

I was so distracted by humming the rest of the verse in my

head that I almost missed what he said next: "We've got a lead on the Scene!"

Sitting up, I blinked, momentarily picturing Trevor staring at a landscape painting in a museum. "Um, the Scene?" I echoed.

"That under-twenty-one club near here?" he said. "I told you about it, remember?"

Oh right. Now I did. "Sure, the Scene," I said. "What do you mean, a lead?"

"Zach was talking to this girl who works at his dentist's office or something, and she told him her cousin's friend knows a guy who takes tickets at the Scene on weekends."

He was talking kind of fast, and I wasn't sure I totally followed. But whatever. The point was, he sounded happy. "That's great," I said. "So you think this dentist chick or whoever can get you some shows at the club?"

"Fingers crossed. If we got a couple of gigs there, it could really open things up for us."

He sounded so excited that it made me smile. Well, smile even harder than I already was just from talking to him. He took his band superseriously, and I just knew they were destined for the big time. Which was awesome. I mean, how cool would it be—me, the girlfriend of a rock god? Especially one as sweet as Trevor?

"I'm sure you'll get those gigs," I told him. "You guys are amazing, and soon the whole world will know it."

"Thanks." I could almost hear him grinning through the phone. "You're amazing too, Chloe."

"Yeah, I know." I twirled a curl around my finger. "It's a gift."

He chuckled. "Anyway, I should probably go. I just wanted to share the big news in person."

"What? You can't go yet." I'd sunk back against Gordo again, but now I shot upright. "We barely got a chance to talk! And listen, I was going to tell you about this new kid who came to the meeting, and—"

"Sorry, babe," he cut me off apologetically. "I'm not even supposed to be on the phone right now. My mom and stepdad have really been riding me about my grades lately, and I have a big bio test coming up tomorrow. If I blow it, they'll ground me from rehearsals, and that's not going to happen."

"Totally," I said with a sigh. "I understand. My parents are completely ridic like that about grades and stuff too."

"Yeah. Text you tomorrow?"

"Definitely. Good luck on the test."

"Thanks."

As I hung up, I sighed loudly, wishing he'd been able to talk longer. It wasn't until I set my phone down that I realized once again he hadn't even mentioned his big secret. At least I didn't think he had.

"Maybe that was it?" I murmured.

But no, his bandmate had just gone to the dentist that afternoon—*after* Trevor had texted me that first tantalizing hint. So what was it he'd wanted to tell me, and why hadn't he told me yet?

I picked up the phone, tempted to text him about it. But I held back, not wanting to distract him from his studying. Even future rock gods had to make decent grades, right?

Or not. But Trevor cared about stuff like that, which was just one more thing to love about him. I grabbed Gordo and hugged him. "I mean, it shows Trev's not just gorgeous and talented," I mumbled into the stuffed pig's squishy pink belly. "He's super-smart and responsible, too. Basically, the perfect boyfriend." I paused. "Or almost-boyfriend. Whatever."

Gordo didn't have much to say, so I tossed him back by my pillows and hopped to my feet. Grabbing my phone again, I plugged it into the tiny set of speakers on my desk and turned on the music app. Trevor had sent me a demo of his band playing "True Romance" a while back, which I'd listened to about a million times since. And I was ready to hear it at least a million more. Setting it on repeat, I flopped back onto my bed and smiled as the familiar first riff rang out.

When Trevor's raspy voice came in, I closed my eyes, wondering how I got so lucky. If my parents had never signed me up for that camp, if Trevor hadn't been there at that same session, if we hadn't both found that music site . . .

"But we did," I murmured. "Because it was fate."

That was another line from the bridge of the song—*Fate is king / It knows what you need / True love is written in the stars. . . .*

I smiled, waiting for the line to come on. Just as the bridge started, though, my phone rang. Or actually, the song cut out, replaced by the theme from The Twilight Zone: Kaz's current ringtone.

"Grr," I muttered, cursing his timing.

But I silenced the music app and picked up. "This better be important," I said. "You just interrupted an awesome daydream."

"Okay," Kaz said uncertainly. "Should I call back later?"

"No, it's fine. I'm kidding." Sort of, anyway. I shifted the phone to my other ear. "What's up?" For a second I felt nervous, sure he was going to bring up that kiss on the cheek again. Definitely weird. Since when did Kaz make me nervous? Like, ever?

"I was just thinking about my party," he said. "I was thinking maybe we should just have, like, a small party at my house."

"Really?" I was relieved—and more than a little surprised by what he'd said. Usually Kaz is pretty adventurous, which means we've done some wacky stuff for his birthday over the years. "I'm sure we can come up with something more interesting than that."

"No, seriously," he insisted. "It's what I want. You know—marking the milestone with just my closest friends and family around in a low-key sort of way . . ."

He did sound serious. I shrugged. "Your wish is our command, I guess. Small, intimate gathering it is. Can we at least dress up for it, though?"

I could practically hear him grin through the phone. "Is the pope Catholic?"

"Cool. That's settled, then."

When Kaz says "low-key," it's probably not exactly how most people would define that term. More like "only fifty of his closest friends and some really great tunes" rather than "epic blowout." So, still fun.

But I wasn't really thinking about the birthday party anymore. My mind was wandering back to the whole awkward kiss reaction. I didn't like thinking about that, so I decided it was time to put us back on normal ground before things got any weirder. I twirled a stray curl around my finger. "So, guess who called me earlier?" I said playfully. "During dinner, actually."

"The president?" Kaz guessed. "Mick Jagger? The aforementioned pope?"

"Wrong, wrong, and wrong."

"Too bad," he said. "But hey, if Mick does happen to call, could you get his autograph for me?"

"Mick who?" I joked, just to annoy him. "But no, seriously, listen. It was Trevor!"

"Oh."

"Yeah." I shivered, remembering how great it had been to see Trevor's name pop up on my phone again. "Anyway, he was calling with big news—his band might get to play at this cool under-twenty-one club near his town soon. I bet once people start hearing them, they'll get superfamous."

"Okay." Kaz cleared his throat. "Listen, I should go."

Uh-oh. He sounded weird again. Had I really freaked him out this much with that silly kiss?

"Are you sure?" I said. "I mean, we could do some planning if you want."

"Tomorrow, okay?" He sounded more normal now. "I haven't called Vanessa yet, or Maya, and I want to make sure the gang from the sci-fi club can make it on Saturday. . . ."

"Oh okay, sure," I said. "See you at school tomorrow."

After I hung up, I stared at the phone in my hand—Kaz's name still on the screen—feeling troubled. Since when did Kaz react so strongly to me doing something goofy like that impulsive kiss? He hadn't thought it, you know, *meant* anything, had he? No way—I was with Trevor. At least, I was pretty sure I was.

Besides, Kaz and I weren't like that. We'd never even thought about turning our friendship into something more, even if Maya liked to tease us by calling us Mr. and Mrs. Band Nerd sometimes.

Trying not to worry about it, I started Trevor's song again from the beginning. Then I leaned back and closed my eyes, the image of Trevor's face filling my mind as the familiar notes washed over me again.

"So, I ordered the pizzas last night, and the Aesop's guy promised to deliver them at eleven tomorrow, which means they should be there by around noon. Maya promised to pick up soda and stuff on her way over." I ticked off the items on my fingers. "And, Vanessa, you got the napkins, right?"

"Right," Vanessa said. "Dad had about a million packages

in the basement from his last trip to Costco. Mom practically begged me to take some."

Kaz grinned. "I always knew his Costco habit would come in handy someday."

It was Friday, and the three of us were in homeroom. Our teacher, Mr. Ortiz, was totally old-school and insisted on seating us in alphabetical order. But thanks to our last names—Aratani, Bell, Bennett—we still ended up sitting together. It had always been that way all through school. We liked to joke it was our own little beginning-of-the-alphabet club. Just one more sign we were destined to be friends.

"Good, then I think everything's under control," I said. "Can't believe we pulled this whole birthday bash together in, like, two days, especially at the same time we're getting ready for the dance marathon."

"Yeah," Kaz said. "Want to come over after school to set up? The place is a mess."

That probably wasn't true, since the Aratanis' housekeeper always came on Thursdays. Still, I nodded. "Sounds like a plan."

"I'm in," Vanessa added. She glanced up as Mr. Ortiz stalked into the room, sweeping his suspicious gaze around at all of us.

I smiled back innocently and then pulled out my phone, knowing it would be my last chance to check it until the first-period bell. The only text was from Maya, checking in about the party plans.

"Hoping for a good-morning text from Trevor?" Vanessa guessed with a smile.

Kaz rolled his eyes. "I thought Trevbo was supposed to be some kind of rock star type," he quipped. "Don't they always sleep till noon?"

"Only the ones who are, like, a hundred years old, like all your idols," I told him. I was relieved he seemed to be over whatever had been making him act so oddly the other day. Focusing on my phone again, I quickly texted Maya back.

Vanessa leaned over for a peek at the screen. When she saw who I was texting, she looked disappointed. "I don't care what Kaz says. I think it's so sweet when Trevor texts you just to say hi," she told me. "Hey, that reminds me—did you ever find out what his big secret was the other day?"

I blinked. "Actually, I sort of forgot about that," I admitted. Between all the party planning, my worries over Kaz being weird, and everything else that was going on, I'd been too busy to think about Trevor's mysterious comment earlier in the week. Scrolling back over our last few text exchanges, I realized he hadn't even hinted about it since then.

"Bulldog Bell actually forgot to find out something she wanted to know?" Kaz feigned extreme shock. "Wow, this guy has you even more twitterpated than I realized!"

"Twitterpated?" I tilted my head at him.

"It's a word," he replied. "Didn't you ever see *Bambi*?"

"Yeah, maybe when I was five." I shrugged. "Anyway, I'm

definitely not twitterpated, whatever that means."

Vanessa smiled. "I've seen Bambi," she said. "One of the kids I babysit for wants to watch it practically every time I come over. And *twitterpated* just means you're head over heels in love."

"Oh." I giggled. "Um, okay, then. Guilty as charged?"

Kaz let out a snort. "Oh man. This guy really *has* turned you into a pod person from Planet Romance, hasn't he?" He leaned over and knocked lightly on my forehead with his knuckles. "Earth to pod person! Please release my friend—you're not fooling anyone!"

I slapped his hand away, not bothering to respond. How could I even begin to explain how Trevor made me feel? It was like that line in "True Romance:" *Nobody gets it until they've been there / It's a feeling that's special, one just we two share. . . .*

As the song said, there was no way to explain that to someone who hadn't felt it. I hadn't even understood it until it had happened to me. Kaz would just have to wait—he'd get it someday when *he* fell in love. Vanessa, too.

In any case, now that I'd remembered Trevor's comments from the other day, my curiosity roared back in full force. I started a new text to him.

Hey, T! Happy Friday! I just remembered u never told me your big secret or whatever. Spill it already! I'm dying of curiosity. U wouldn't want me to be totally distracted for K's bday party tomorrow, right?

I smiled and hit send. "There," I said. "Hopefully, he'll text me back soon."

"He'd better," Kaz said. "Or he won't know what hit him."

Vanessa laughed. "Yeah, once our Chloe decides she wants something, she won't stop until she gets it."

"Or dies trying," Kaz agreed.

Just then Mr. Ortiz called the class to order. "Pipe down, people," he growled. "Announcements."

I traded an eye roll with my friends. Our school's morning announcements could be a cure for insomnia. Usually all we get is the school secretary droning on for several minutes about the lunch menu and the sports team schedules. Maybe the occasional fire drill for some real excitement.

As usual I zoned out as the announcements started, slipping into more daydreams about Trevor. Could he be getting ready to declare his love, like "True Romance" said? If so, why was he being so slow about it?

Maybe he's waiting for a good reason, I thought. Do we have an anniversary coming up or something?

I started counting back in my head. I knew it had been at least three months since I'd recognized him in that video. Could he be aiming his declaration for our four-month anniversary? When was that, anyway? Let's see, it had been a Tuesday afternoon—or was it a Wednesday . . . ?

"Ow," I blurted out, yanked out of my calculations by a hard poke in the arm, courtesy of Vanessa.

"Did you hear that?" she whispered.

"Hear what?" I glared at her, rubbing the sore spot on my arm.

She tilted her head toward the speaker. The secretary was still droning on. But I blinked as I heard her say the word *dance.*

"Was that about the dance marathon?" I asked.

"No. There's going to be a *school* dance," Vanessa whispered, shooting a glance toward Mr. Ortiz to make sure he didn't notice us talking. "In two weeks!"

"Really?" That was huge news. Our school isn't big on dances. Normally we have the prom for juniors and seniors, homecoming for everybody, and maybe one more dance around Valentine's Day. So this was new.

"A dance, huh?" Kaz whispered. "Great, I'll be able to get myself all warmed up for it at the dance marathon!" He shimmied in his seat, his long arms and legs all going in different directions.

Finally the announcements ended, which meant we were allowed to talk out loud again. Vanessa immediately spun to face me. "This is huge," she said, her blue eyes glowing. "A dance! Fun, right?"

I grinned. She's such a romantic! She's the one who always drags us to all the new chick flicks, even though Kaz and I prefer a good comedy or action movie. Or pretty much anything but a chick flick, for that matter.

"Totally fun," I agreed. "Not to mention potentially romantic." I waggled my eyebrows at her. "We'll have to get right to work landing you a hot date, hmm?"

She looked alarmed. "Oh, I don't know. I was thinking the three of us could all go together like we usually do."

"Not if we can hook you up with Mr. Right by then." My smile faded as I realized something. "Too bad we won't be able to double-date. Not with my own Mr. Right a zillion miles away."

Kaz rolled his eyes. "Yeah, bummer."

"It *is* a bummer," I said. "But I'll just have to throw all my energy into living vicariously through Vanessa's big romantic evening."

She giggled, her cheeks going pink. "Stop," she said. "Still, it's going to be fun, right? Too bad Trevor can't come here for the big night, though."

"I know, right?" For half a second I allowed myself to daydream. But then I shook my head. "Maybe next year when he has his license . . ." My smile crept back, and as the bell rang I allowed myself to sink into another daydream. Okay, this one was set far in the future—a whole year away. But true romance was worth waiting for, right? That was what the song said, anyway.

That afternoon Vanessa's mom picked us up from school and dropped all three of us at Kaz's house. It was quiet and deserted when we walked in—his dad was at the office, as usual.

"Okay." Vanessa rubbed her hands together, surveying the spotless living room. "What should we do first?"

I looked around too. The entire first floor of Kaz's house has looked pretty much exactly the same for as long as I can remember. He told me once his mom had decorated it, and his dad didn't want to change anything. At least that's what his other relatives think. It should have been cozy, with lots of overstuffed furniture and a stack of magazines on the coffee table, but it always felt a little sterile to me. Maybe because that was all there was—furniture and magazines. No dog lying around on the rug. No family pictures on the walls or the big stone mantel. Not even a houseplant. The piano in the corner looked as if nobody ever touched it, even though I knew Kaz played it sometimes.

"First of all, let's liven up the place a little," I suggested. "Otherwise, nobody's going to know this is a party. Where's the decoration stuff?"

Vanessa had raided her dad's Costco stash for some of the raw materials we planned to use to turn Boring Junction into Party Central, and I'd stopped by the local party store after school the day before for more. Vanessa is the art teacher's favorite student ever, so she'd been able to snag some additional stuff from the supply closet at school. We had plenty to work with.

"What did you guys get?" Kaz asked, peering into one of the bags we'd grabbed from the trunk of Van's mom's car. "Streamers and balloons? Very original."

"I prefer the term *classic*," I retorted. "Come on. Let's get started."

Kaz brightened. "I'll put on some decorating music."

"No!" I howled, throwing myself in his path as he headed for his dad's old-school stereo system. "This may be your house and your birthday, but we are so not listening to Gregorian chants or whatever you had in mind."

Kaz smiled. "Dixieland jazz, actually."

I wasn't sure if he was serious or not, and I didn't bother to ask. "But never fear, I made us a playlist during study hall." I whipped out my phone. "Voila!"

I punched it on, and the familiar strains of "True Romance" poured out.

Kaz rolled his eyes. "Seriously?"

Vanessa was already humming along. "You should have used Trevor's band's version." She glanced at Kaz. "Have you heard it yet? It's really good."

"I'm sure." Kaz leaned over and forwarded to the next song, an old reggae tune we all liked. "Okay, that's more like it. Let's get to work!"

For the next half hour we worked on turning the bland living room into a work of art. Or at least making it more fun. We strung streamers over the lamps and curtains, made a balloon bouquet for the table, and even hung up a fake disco ball—Kaz especially loved that part.

I was arranging a bunch of flameless candles on top of the piano when the buzz of a familiar ringtone broke through the song that was playing at the moment. "That's Trevor!" I blurted out, almost tripping over Vanessa as I lunged for the phone. "He finally texted me back. It's about time!"

We'd been having so much fun, I hadn't had time to dwell on the fact that Trevor still hadn't responded to the text I'd sent him in homeroom. But now he was all I could think about as I eagerly scanned the message.

Hey, C, got your text. Sorry, I totally forgot about that. Wish I hadn't said anything, actually, bc it's not happening after all.

I blinked, waiting for another text to appear. Five long seconds later the screen was still blank, so I quickly texted back.

What's not happening???

"What did he say?" Vanessa peered over my shoulder.

"Nothing much yet," I replied, tapping my foot as I waited for the response.

It finally came.

Lol, relax, I was about to tell u. I thought I might be back there in my old stomping grounds in a week or so for a family reunion and we could maybe get together or whatever. But my mom and her sister got in a huge fight, so now we're not coming after all.

My eyes widened, and I let out a gasp. "Oh my gosh! He was coming here?"

My thumbs flew over the keyboard. *Are you sure you're not coming? That would be amazing!!!!!!!!!!*

Again it seemed to take forever before his response came, though it was probably only an hour or two. Or a few seconds, I guess.

I know, right? Oh well, maybe they'll make up by next year's reunion, lol! Gtg. The guys are waiting to get started. Later!

I stared at the screen, so overwhelmed by what he'd just told me that I couldn't speak for a moment. Which, if you know me, is really saying something.

Finally even Kaz noticed my freak-out and wandered over.

"What's going on?" he asked. "Did Trevor break a guitar string or something?"

Vanessa shot him a look. "Be nice," she said. "Trevor just told Chloe he was almost going to come to town. Well, his town. Whatever."

"Close enough," I said, finally finding my voice. "I can't believe this! How amazing would that have been?"

But it wasn't going to happen, and I was devastated. Okay, so I hadn't been expecting it to happen anytime soon, but that wasn't the point. Because now I knew it *could* have happened, but it wouldn't. Which was a horrible feeling.

Vanessa was watching me, her blue eyes soft with sympathy. "Maybe he'll come another time," she said, giving me a hug.

"I don't know. It's probably just as well." Kaz already seemed to be losing interest; he'd picked up a roll of streamers and was eyeing the chandelier in the dining room. "I mean, what kind of future could you two have anyway with him living so far away? You should probably find someone closer."

As he wandered off, I sighed and traded a shrug with Vanessa. Kaz was so not a romantic—he just didn't get it. And I definitely wasn't in the mood to try to break it down for him just then.

"Come on," I said heavily, switching back to the music app. "We'd better finish up here."

Chapter Four

"Hold still—I don't want to poke your eye out." Vanessa leaned toward me, the tip of her tongue sticking out like it always did when she concentrated.

I held my breath, trying not to flinch as the eyeliner pencil came at me. Soon she'd drawn a perfect cat's eye in glitter green on each lid. I glanced in the mirror and smiled.

"Perfect," I said, blinking my suddenly much more exotic eyes. "Now I definitely look ready to party."

"Good. Now do me." Vanessa handed me a gray pencil and perched on the edge of her bed. "But nothing too crazy, okay?"

"I get it." I winked. "You want to look pretty in case any of the guys at the party turn out to be your dream date for the big dance.

Don't worry. I'll make you look perfect. Well, even more perfect than usual, that is."

It was Saturday morning, Kaz's birthday. My dad had dropped me off at Vanessa's around ten, which we figured would give us plenty of time to get all dolled up for the party. Vanessa's mom was driving us to Kaz's place soon.

We'd already dressed up—Vanessa in a long, floaty floral dress, and me in sparkly leggings and a cool blinged-out tunic. Okay, so it was just a casual get-together in the middle of the day. So what? The anniversary of Kaz's birth was a special occasion, and that called for special outfits. At least in our opinion.

When Vanessa's face was done, I stood up and twirled in front of the full-length mirror hanging on the back of her bedroom door. "Do we look ready to party or what?" I exclaimed. "Come here. I want to get a picture of us to send to Trevor." I frowned slightly. "Especially since it's the only way he'll get to see me, thanks to his cranky relatives."

Okay, so I hadn't quite recovered from Trevor's news yet—so sue me. It had only been, like, eighteen and a half hours. Not that I was counting.

Vanessa joined me in front of the mirror, and we struck a pose. I snapped several photos and then texted the best of them to Trevor.

"There," I said. "That'll give him a taste of what he's missing."

Vanessa shot me a sympathetic look. "I still can't believe he was going to be so close so soon."

"Tell me about it." I'd only been dwelling on that very fact for the past eighteen and a half hours. Well, eighteen hours and forty-two minutes now, actually. "And you know what I realized? He said a week or two, right?" I took a deep breath. "What if he'd actually been here for the school dance?"

Vanessa gasped, her carefully lined eyes going round and dismayed. "Oh, I hadn't even thought of that! How romantic would that be?"

"Yeah." I sighed. "It would be straight out of the song, actually—remember that line?"

"You'll know it's true on a magical night, whether sailing at sea or dancing in the moonlight," Vanessa sang softly. "Oh, Chloe. I'm so sorry."

She looked so devastated that I almost giggled. "It's okay. I'll live. Probably." I hummed the next line of the song, which happened to be the one about special first kisses: *That's when you'll share a first kiss if you dare / Remember it always: true romance is rare.* Oh well. Maybe next year . . .

At that moment Van's mother's voice drifted up to us, calling our names.

"Oops." Vanessa checked her watch. "Time to go."

We were in the car when my phone buzzed again. It was Trevor.

Hey, cutie, just checking in before I meet up with the guys in a few. Saw your pic—very nice! Why are u guys so dressed up? Got a hot date today? Lol! Anyway, wanted to check in since I'll probably be out of touch for hours—we're auditioning drummers today, remember? Hope u have a great day!

I did remember, though I guessed from his comment about our outfits that he didn't remember today was Kaz's party. Oh well—he had a lot on his mind. The band had put out a bunch of online ads for a new drummer, and tons of people had responded. Which just went to show how famous Of Note was already getting, at least in their local music scene.

I texted him back: *Good luck with the auditions! I'll be at K's party all day myself, but text me later, okay? Bye!* ☺

He texted back a moment later: *U know it! Tell K happy bday from me.*

Just then Vanessa's mom pulled over to the curb in front of Kaz's house. "Have fun, girls," she said.

"Thanks, Mom." Van smiled at me. "Ready to get this party started?"

I stuck my phone into my pocket. "Let's go."

By twelve thirty, Kaz's living room was packed. Pretty much every single person we'd invited had shown up, which should have been surprising, given the last-minute invitations. But for Kaz? No surprise at all, really. People liked him. Enough to change their plans, even.

I was returning from fetching more napkins from the kitchen when I paused to look around, a little amazed as always at the variety of Kaz's friends and admirers. The entire sci-fi club had turned out, along with his friends from various other clubs and classes, including the popular president of the sophomore class. Speaking of über-popular people, Maya was over near the punch bowl chatting with a couple of random people. She never traveled without an entourage, and today she'd brought her current boyfriend and a couple of her fellow cheerleaders. And of course at least half the music department was there—that practically went without saying. Kaz was into a lot of stuff, but music was his first love. Just one more reason we got along so well.

"This is fun." A kid named Wallace wandered over to me, clutching a plastic cup of punch. "Okay, maybe not as cool as the laser tag party I wanted Kaz to do, but hey."

I didn't bother to explain that Kaz himself had requested a quieter, more low-key party this year. Which this qualified as, at least in Kaz's world. I dropped the napkins onto the coffee table and smiled at Wallace, sizing him up. He was one of the cuter nerds from the sci-fi club, with adorably messy dark hair and a brain like a calculator. Would he make a suitable dance date for Vanessa? Maybe even turn out to be her Dream Nerd so she could be as happy as Trevor and I were?

"Yeah, glad you made it," I said. "So, did you hear about the school dance? Big news, huh?"

Before Wallace could respond, Kaz's father stuck his head in from the front hallway. "Everything going all right in here, kids?" he called out.

"Yeah, great," I told him as everybody else nodded or saluted him with their plastic cups. "Want some punch, Dr. A?"

Dr. Aratani smiled, which as always made him look like Kaz's older, sadder, wearier ghost. "Thanks, but I have to go to the office and take care of some paperwork," he said. "I know I can trust you kids to behave, hmm?"

"Sure, Dad." Kaz pasted a big, fake grin onto his face. "We totally won't roll out the beer keg until you've left the driveway."

Dr. Aratani rolled his eyes. "Happy birthday, son."

Kaz's smile faded into something more sincere, if a touch sad. "Thanks, Dad."

Dr. Aratani waved to the rest of us and disappeared. I glanced at Kaz, who was still staring at the spot where his father had been.

"Come on," I said, linking my arm through his. "Let's dance. We need to practice for the marathon, right?"

A few people heard me and cheered, and Maya's friend Toni actually did a little cheerleadery leap and a fist pump. "Dance marathon, yeah!" she cried.

Maya's boyfriend, a stout senior wrestler appropriately nicknamed Tank, hooted at her. "Tone it down, Tonester!" he exclaimed.

"Leave her alone." Maya gave him a shove, though the effect resembled a flea shoving a brick wall. "She's just psyched about the marathon."

"We all are," I said. "It's going to be a blast. And remember, it was all Kaz's brilliant idea."

"Thank you, thank you." Kaz swept into a dramatic bow. "But I couldn't have pulled it together without all the little people who believed in my genius."

"We haven't pulled it together yet, genius boy," Maya reminded him. She glanced around the room. "Don't forget there's another planning meeting tomorrow for the fund-raiser, people. Be there, okay? We have a ton to do and only another week to do it all."

"Okay," one of the trombone players said. "But today we're supposed to be having fun, remember? Not working on the fund-raiser."

"We can do both!" Kaz shimmied his hips. "Come on, everyone—let's practice our moves!"

Vanessa laughed and cranked up the music. Kaz started spazzing out on the dance floor, finally leaping over and dragging Maya out to dance with him. She laughed and started grooving, barely seeming worried about her cousin's limbs flying around and threatening to clock her.

I grinned, my own foot already tapping to the rhythm. "Come on," I said, grabbing Vanessa. "Let's get out there."

We must have danced for an hour. At some point, despite my carefully selected playlist, Kaz took over the music. Everyone ended up doing the hokey pokey for a while, then disco dancing, then switching to square dancing when Kaz selected some ancient country-western song. That was fun, but it was nothing compared to trying to keep up with the wacked-out, breakneck rhythm when Kaz dug up a vinyl copy of "Sabre Dance" by

Khachaturian—one of our favorite love-to-hate it numbers from the school band. The clarinet part is brutal but also kind of fun.

Finally, though, my legs were ready to fall off. I stumbled away from the dance floor, leaving everyone else to face Kaz's next challenge—moonwalking to some old Michael Jackson.

Vanessa followed me out to the dining room. "This is fun, right?" she said breathlessly.

I gulped down half a cup of punch before I answered. "Yeah. What else would you expect from a Kazuo Aratani joint?" I shot her a sidelong look. "By the way, what do you think of that guy Wallace?"

"Why do you ask?" she said cautiously.

I smiled innocently. "Why do you think?"

Just then Maya hurried in, her face flushed and her perky ponytail slightly askew. "Hey, ladies," she said, dipping a cup into the punch bowl. "What are we talking about over here? Any fun gossip?"

"I was just trying to convince Van she totally needs a hot date for the dance," I told Maya. "Can you help me talk some sense into her?"

"Please don't," Vanessa protested. "Seriously, Chloe. Just because you're sort of dating a future rock star and you think everyone needs to be paired up now . . ."

"Chloe's dating someone? Hold up—did I miss something?" Maya went all sharp and interested, zeroing in on me like a laser. "Kaz didn't tell me you had a boyfriend, Chloe."

"Sort of." I pulled out my phone. "His name's Trevor. Want to see?"

"Absolutely." She watched as I scrolled through my photos, and then grabbed the phone when I held it out, studying the picture I'd chosen—one Trevor had sent of him posing with his favorite guitar. "Very nice," Maya declared after a moment.

"Thanks." I watched as she scrolled around, checking out a few other pictures Trevor had sent of himself. "He's really cool." I went on to give her the short version of how Trevor and I got together, a little surprised Kaz had never mentioned him to her. He and Maya are pretty close—he has dinner at her house at least once a week.

When I finished, she returned the phone and picked up her punch again. "Wow, that's crazy you found each other online." She paused to take a sip. "I hope Kaz isn't jealous, though."

"What are you talking about? Jealous of what?"

Maya set her cup down again and shrugged, reaching up to adjust her ponytail. "I guess I just sort of assumed you and Kaz would end up together, Chloe."

"Huh?" I shot a look at Vanessa, who looked perplexed. But for some reason I was flashing back yet again to that awkwardness after the kiss. Was I totally sending out the wrong signals somehow, making everyone think I wanted to get all romantic with Kaz? Maybe including Kaz himself? If so, no wonder he'd looked at me like I was crazy! "Kaz and I are just friends, Maya—you know that," I said firmly. "Best friends, but just friends."

"Okay." She glanced into the living room, where Kaz was the center of attention as he danced on the piano bench. "Still. Best friends turn into more than friends all the time, right?"

"Not us," I said quickly.

But she wasn't finished. "And you two are perfect together. You get along great, you spend all your time together. . . ." She smiled as Kaz fell off the bench, almost taking Toni's head off on his way down. Good thing the girl has quick reflexes from all those years of cheering. "You even have the same weird sense of humor."

I wasn't sure how to respond to that. Part of me wanted to laugh it off, tell her she was nuts. But for some reason, part of me was thinking about it. Kaz, me, together? Would that really work?

Before I could come up with a coherent response, Tank wandered past and spotted Maya. "Get over here, woman!" he bellowed. "I want to dance!"

She rolled her eyes. "Keep your pants on, man. I'm coming." She hurried toward him.

"That was weird," I said when she was gone, still not quite ready to let it go. "Why would Maya even think something like that?"

"I don't know." Vanessa took a sip of punch. "But don't worry about it. I mean, Maya has dated, like, a zillion guys, right?" She watched as Tank spun Maya around out on the dance floor. "She probably isn't used to having guys as just friends, you know?"

"You're probably right." My gaze shifted from Maya to Kaz, who was wandering toward the dining room. "Too bad for her—she doesn't know what she's missing. Am I right?"

With a sudden rush of fondness, I hurried forward to meet Kaz with a hug. I was being ridiculous to worry about something that was definitely all in Maya's mind. "Having fun, birthday boy?"

He hugged me back, then looked down, his brown eyes a bit startled. I gulped, sort of wishing I'd stuck to a high-five or something. Would I ever learn?

"Um, yeah," he mumbled. He leaned closer, staring at me with a weird expression on his face.

My heart thumped as I flashed back to what Maya had just said. What would it be like? It would be so easy right now—all I'd have to do was stand up on my tiptoes, grab his face, pull his lips toward mine. . . .

I yanked away from him before my crazy little fantasy could go any further, spinning around toward the punch bowl. "Have some punch!" I exclaimed, my voice ringing a little too loudly in my own ears.

Whoa. I had to get a grip! Glancing over my shoulder, I saw Kaz looked kind of confused now. No wonder—I was acting like a psycho.

"Sure, thanks, Chloe," he said. "That's kind of why I came in here."

I laughed, trying to reset my mood from "weirded out" to

"normal." Kaz and I were friends, and that was more than enough. Anything else I'd just been thinking had to come from a combination of Trevor's disappointing news, Maya's deluded comments, and my usual party mania.

Handing Kaz his punch, I tapped my foot to the beat of the current pop song currently playing out in the living room—obviously someone had taken over DJ duty from Kaz. "Hurry up and chug it, dude," I said. "I feel like dancing."

Chapter Five

A few hours later the party was finally winding down. A bunch of people had left already, and others were doing the getting-ready-to-leave thing—hovering near the door, carrying their used cups and dirty napkins to the kitchen, and looking around for lost shoes or phones or purses or whatever.

Maya was flopped on the sofa, talking to Tank and Toni and a few people from band. They didn't seem to be in any hurry to leave, which was another hallmark of Kaz's parties. Several other band members were at the piano, where one of them was using his finger to pick out the tune to one of our band numbers.

Kaz was over by the windows, deep in a passionate argument about Star Trek with Wallace and another guy from the sci-fi club, who also happened to play percussion in band. I thought about going over and joining in, but decided I didn't feel that strongly about *Original Series* vs. *Next Generation* at the moment. Or ever, really.

Noticing Vanessa taking a seat beside the others on the sofa, I headed over to join them too. They were talking about the S&D fund-raiser.

"And Mr. Graves talked the janitorial staff into letting the marathon go until seven, even though they usually lock everything up by five on Sundays," she was saying when I walked over, sounding pleased.

"Cool," one of Van's fellow flute players said, nodding so enthusiastically that her dreadlocks bounced.

"Wait." Tank's massive forehead was folded into a puzzled expression. "I thought it was a marathon. Like, dance until you drop? Isn't that how it works?"

Kaz wandered over just in time to hear him. "Yeah, that was my original idea," he said, grinning. "You just keep dancing until your legs fall off. People would pay to see that, right? Totally Christians vs. lions."

"Yeah, except bloodier, at least if *you're* one of the dancers." Maya rolled her eyes. "Don't worry, I'm sure the modified version will still provide plenty of entertainment."

"Especially if we let Kaz dance!" one of the sci-fi girls added with a laugh.

Vanessa laughed too. "Think of the children!" she exclaimed, putting a hand to her forehead in mock despair.

"Sorry to disappoint." Kaz smiled at all of us. "My services are required in band, I'm afraid. But maybe I can sneak in one Watusi or something at the end."

I grinned and then glanced at Tank, who still looked confused. "Our marathon's still going to last for hours," I told him. "Pretty much all day, actually. The idea is that volunteers from band will play dance music, and people can donate money to dance with a cheerleader or a cute S&D kid."

Toni nodded. "Plus we're all signing up people to sponsor us," she added. "The longer we can keep going, the more money we'll make that way too."

"At least until seven p.m.," Vanessa put in.

"Oh." Tank looked at Maya. "Is that what you made me sign the other day?"

She smiled sweetly. "I explained it to you then, babe," she said. "Don't worry. I only put you down for ten dollars per hour."

Everyone laughed as Tank looked alarmed.

"This is going to be fun," one of the other band girls said. "Thanks for the idea, Kaz."

"Yeah," Toni put in. "Definitely an improvement over some stupid car wash or whatever."

Kaz jumped to his feet and bowed. "You're very welcome," he said. "I can't wait to serenade my lovely cousin and her peppy friends all day long."

By then everyone in the room was listening to the conversation, including the band members over by the piano. "Speaking of serenading people, I think we forgot something at this party," one of them said.

She started picking out "Happy Birthday to You" on the piano. A few people started to sing along. But Kaz dove for the hall, returning a moment later holding his trumpet.

"That's not how you play 'Happy Birthday,'" he declared with a grin. "This is how you play 'Happy Birthday'!"

He started to blow, swinging into a jazzy version of the familiar tune. This time almost everyone started singing or humming along. Tank even drummed out a steady rhythm on the coffee table.

I laughed and darted out into the hall, immediately spotting Kaz's clarinet case sticking half out of the closet where he usually kept it. It took me only a few seconds to fit the instrument together and moisten the reed. Then I hurried back into the room, joining in with some sick harmony.

"Go, Chloe!" Maya shouted, shooting me a thumbs-up.

I joined Kaz in the middle of the room. A guy named Bill who plays the organ at his church had already taken over from the first girl and was playing full out on the piano, his hands flying up and down the keys like a pro. Tank was still drumming along, and everyone else was whistling or singing. Basically, it was a full-on jam session.

When we all got tired of "Happy Birthday to You," we switched to "When the Saints Go Marching In." Maya, Toni, and a few others got up and danced, clearly channeling some wild Mardi Gras parade. Kaz leaped to the head of the line, dancing as he played, which made me laugh so hard, I couldn't continue playing myself. One of the other clarinetists grabbed the instrument from me, taking over while I collapsed onto the sofa next to Vanessa, who was singing in her clear soprano voice.

"This is fun, isn't it?" she said, interrupting herself.

I smiled and leaned my head on her shoulder, catching my breath. "Yeah."

Then I felt something vibrate in my pocket. It was my phone—the music was so loud, I hadn't heard the text tone. Pulling it out, I saw it was a message from Trevor.

I hesitated, glancing at the raucous parade, itching to join in. Trevor knew I was busy today; he wouldn't mind if I checked in with him later. . . .

But curiosity got the better of me. Trevor was supposed to be busy all day too. Why was he texting me?

"Be right back," I told Vanessa.

I hurried out to the kitchen, wanting a little privacy. Opening the text, I scanned it.

Hey, C! What's up? Figured I'd check in while we're taking a break. The next drummer is due in, like, five. But there's probably no point in seeing anyone else—we just auditioned this totally awesome drummer, and I'm pretty sure she's going to be the one.

I blinked, my gaze catching on that word: *she*. "A chick drummer, huh?" I murmured.

Interesting. Not that I was going to freak out about it, though. I didn't want to be *that* almost-girlfriend. The one who got all jealous when her guy was friends with other girls. No way, that so wasn't me.

"Is it Trevor?"

I looked up, realizing Vanessa had followed me into the kitchen without my even hearing her. No wonder. The ruckus in the next room had gotten even louder as everyone switched over to our school fight song. It would be a miracle if the neighbors didn't call the cops. Then again probably not. They all loved Kaz too.

"Yeah, it's Trevor." I showed her the text. "Guess they found their new drummer."

"It's a girl?" Vanessa shot me a surprised look. "Are you okay with that? I thought the band was all guys."

I shrugged. "So now there's a girl. It's no biggie. Trevor is into me, not her."

Vanessa smiled. "Good for you. You have no reason to feel threatened. I mean, you and Trevor are obviously meant for each other, right?"

"Right. Like the song says." I started singing the chorus of "True Romance," and Vanessa joined in.

"True romance, it's the air that we breathe. Just us two together, yeah, just you and me."

I smiled, tapping out a quick response to Trevor. Then I pocketed my phone, and Vanessa and I hurried back out to rejoin the fun.

An hour and a half later everyone had gone home except me and Vanessa.

"Where do you want this?" I asked Kaz as I pulled down the

disco ball. I twirled it around on its string, enjoying the way its cheap aluminum foil facets caught the light.

Kaz looked over from picking potato chip crumbs out of the rug. "Don't throw that out!" he said. "I want to hang it over my bed."

"You would," Vanessa said with a laugh. "By the way, Chloe and I totally didn't mean for that silly thing to be your only birthday gift. You never told us what you wanted, though."

I lowered the disco ball, realizing she was right. "Yeah, now or never, dude," I told Kaz. "What do you want? I know! We could take you to that display of antique musical instruments at the museum. I think it started last weekend, right?"

Vanessa wrinkled her nose at me. "What kind of gift is that? The museum has free admission for students, remember?"

"Oh right." I grinned and shrugged. "Well, the gift part would be the pleasure of our company."

Kaz smiled. "That's the only gift I really need," he said. "I would kind of like to see that *show*, actually."

"Fine, but that's not going to be your gift," Vanessa insisted. "Tell us what you want. For real."

Kaz rubbed his hands together. "Actually, I've been thinking about it over the past few days, and there *is* something I want from each of you."

"So spill it already." I set the disco ball on the coffee table and bent to pick up a crumpled napkin poking out from beneath the sofa.

"Okay." He looked at Vanessa. "I volunteered to make the posters for the sci-fi club's next movie night before I remembered I can't even draw a stick figure." He grinned. "So will you help me with them?"

"Sure, I'd love to," Vanessa said immediately.

"What about me?" I asked. "I can't draw either, so I'll be no help with the posters."

"No, I have another idea for you." He took a step toward me, sort of grinning and puffing out his cheeks at the same time.

I tilted my head. "What? You look weird."

He cleared his throat. "Um . . ."

My eyes narrowed as I tried to read his expression. "What are you going to ask me to do?" I said cautiously. "Nothing illegal or immoral or involving big hairy spiders, right?"

"No, nothing like that." He cleared his throat again, his gaze bouncing from me to Vanessa to the floor to the ceiling. "I just thought, well, if you think it's okay, uh—"

"Spit it out already," I said. "What is it?"

He met my eyes again. "I want you to go to the school dance with me," he blurted out in a rush. "As, um, my date."

Chapter Six

For a second I couldn't respond, though I felt my face go red as that little fantasy from earlier popped into my head. Had Kaz sensed I was thinking about kissing him? Was he messing with me?

"You're kidding, right?" I sounded a little panicky, so I cleared my throat and tried again. "I mean, um, what do you mean? We always go to the dances together."

"Right. But this time I want us to go *together* together." He shuffled his feet, still watching me. Then he shifted his gaze to Vanessa. "You don't mind, right?" he added, suddenly sounding worried. "I mean, I know Chloe promised to find you some big romantic date or whatever, but if you were counting on us to—"

"No, it's totally fine," Vanessa cut him off, shooting me an uncertain look. "I can tag along with someone from band. I mean, if Chloe, um . . ." She let her voice trail off and then shrugged helplessly, clearly not sure what I would want her to say.

I took a deep breath, not sure what to say either. Had I started all this with that spur-of-the-moment kiss the other day? Did Kaz think I *wanted* him to ask me?

The weirdest thing was, the fantasy-generating part of my mind was off and running again. Wondering what it would be like. Me and Kaz on a romantic date . . .

That word snapped me out of it: *romantic*. Because it reminded me of "True Romance," which of course reminded me I already had my dream guy.

Still, I didn't want to hurt Kaz's feelings. . . . "Okay, I'm going to need some time to process this," I told Kaz. "Trust me when I say this was *not* what I was expecting you to ask for as a birthday gift."

"That's fine," he said quickly. "I can wait for your answer. No hurry." He grinned. "Well, actually you have a two-week deadline. There's not much point in either answer after the dance is over."

I smiled weakly. "Okay, then. Um . . ."

The faint sound of a car horn drifted through the house from out front. Saved by the bell.

"That's my mom." Van checked her watch. "Right on time, as always."

"Go ahead. We're almost done here anyway." Kaz looked around the room. It wasn't quite back to its usual sterile condition, but it didn't look like a tornado had just rolled through, either. "See you guys at the meeting tomorrow?"

"See you then," I replied, heading for the door without quite meeting his eyes.

"Yeah. Happy birthday, Kaz," Vanessa added.

As soon as we were outside, the door shut behind us, she turned to stare at me. "What was that?" she exclaimed.

"I know, right?" I shook my head as we walked toward her mom's car, which was idling at the curb. "What in the world is he thinking?"

"That he likes you as more than a friend?" Vanessa shrugged. "Maybe Maya was onto something after all."

"Get real."

"I am real," she said. "If you think about it, it really does make sense. You and Kaz have a ton in common. You get along great. You spend all your time together. You make each other laugh until you snort soda out your noses."

"So do you and Kaz," I pointed out. "Not to mention you and me." I spun around and dropped to my knee. "Vanessa, will you go to the dance with me? As, like, my date?"

"Get up, you loon." She kicked me lightly in the knee. "I'm serious about this."

I sighed as I climbed to my feet. She had that dreamy look in her eyes—the one she got when she watched those sappy romantic movies. "Stop," I said.

Too late. "I can see it now," she singsonged, her blue eyes unfocused as if gazing into some rose-tinted future only she could see. "You and Kaz at the dance, slow dancing to the music, realizing this was what you both wanted all along . . . "

"Hold on. Stop right there." I frowned at her. "Aren't you forgetting something? Or rather some*one*? What about Trevor?"

Vanessa blinked, her eyes returning to the here and now. "Oh right," she said. "I did forget about him for a sec." She shrugged and hurried forward to open the car's back door. "I mean, he's superdreamy and all, but he doesn't seem quite real, you know? Living so far away and everything . . . "

"Have fun, girls?" Vanessa's mom looked up from texting as we climbed into the backseat. "I hope Kazuo enjoyed his party."

"He did." Vanessa shot me a look. "He really, really did."

I scowled at her, miming a lip-zip. I so didn't want to talk about this in front of her mom. Or anybody, really. Not until I figured out what was going on and how to deal with it.

As Mrs. Bennett pulled away from the curb, I leaned back against the seat, staring at nothing. Vanessa might not think Trevor was real, but I knew better. I mean, I'd spent two whole weeks with him at music camp. Not to mention talking or texting with him pretty much every day for the past few months.

Besides, who could argue with the way we'd reconnected? It was fate—meant to be. Just like the song said. That was the difference between Kaz and Trevor. Maybe Vanessa didn't get it, but I did.

Closing my eyes, I hummed "True Romance" the rest of the way home.

• • •

That night after dinner I went up to my room and changed into the shorts and T-shirt I usually slept in. I liked to be comfortable for my weekend phone sessions with Trevor, since they often lasted long into the night. I set my phone on my desk and then started my math homework while I waited for Trevor's call. I'd be busy with that fund-raiser planning meeting the next day, and Ms. Feldman didn't accept any excuses for unfinished problem sets. Besides, Trevor was a little late, and some geometry seemed as good a way as any to distract myself while I waited.

Normally I was pretty good at math. But that night the numbers and symbols swam in front of my eyes, refusing to arrange themselves into any patterns that made sense.

Something else that didn't make sense? The recent weirdness between me and Kaz. We were so great as friends. I couldn't even imagine trying to turn that into a romance. Or could I? Maya certainly didn't seem to have any trouble picturing it, and even Vanessa hadn't seemed to find it so strange.

Dropping my pencil, I leaned back in my chair and stared at the ceiling. Kaz wasn't anything like the kind of guy I'd pictured having as a boyfriend someday. Was I missing the romantic potential in the boy next door? Could I even begin to imagine living out the lyrics to "True Romance" with someone like him—good old geeky Kaz?

Suddenly I realized my phone was vibrating, making that impatient little stifled-bee buzz it makes when the ringer is off.

I grabbed the phone, expecting it to be Trevor. But the name over the little telephone icon on the screen was Kazuo Aratani.

With a deep breath, I hit the green button. "Hello?"

"Hey, Chloe," Kaz's familiar voice responded. "Don't panic. I'm not calling to demand an answer from you."

I relaxed and even smiled a little as his familiar snorting laugh rang out over the tiny speaker. "Okay," I said. "So why are you calling?"

"Wanted to make sure your phone was on. I'm texting you a very important picture right now, okay?"

"Okay." I pulled the phone away from my ear. Sure enough, a text popped up a moment later. It was a photo of Kaz striking a *ta-da* pose in front of his shower—where he'd hung the disco ball from the ceiling, several flashlights pointing up at it and making the whole bathroom sparkle.

I laughed. Classic Kaz! "What a nerd," I murmured, shaking my head. Then I put the phone back to my ear. "Very nice," I said. "You'll be able to take the grooviest showers in town."

"Yeah." Kaz sounded pleased with himself. "Okay, better send it to Van next. See you tomorrow."

"Bye." As I hung up, I was still smiling. Kaz always made me laugh, that was for sure. Still, a guy who hung a fake disco ball in his shower? Perfect as a friend, but maybe not so much as my super-romantic knight in shining armor. I just had to remember that and not get myself all confused again.

The phone buzzed again in my hand; I still hadn't turned the ringer back on. I put it to my ear without checking. "Okay, Kaz, what now?" I said.

"Um, Chloe?"

Oops. I realized it wasn't Kaz calling back after all.

"Hi, Trevor," I said. "Sorry. I just hung up with Kaz, and he sent this picture, and, well, never mind." Taking a deep breath, I told myself to focus. "How are you?"

"Fine." He sounded a little confused. No wonder. "Sorry I'm a little late calling you. The band ended up going out for food after rehearsal. We wanted to celebrate and make Zoe feel welcome, you know?"

"Zoe?" I echoed. "I take it that's the new chick drummer you texted about?"

He chuckled. "Oh right, sorry. Yeah, that's her. It's weird—she's been in the band only about five minutes, but it's already like she fits right in."

"That's cool." I got up from my desk and flopped onto my bed.

"Yeah, she's an amazing drummer, and she really gets our sound. We think she's exactly what the band needs to finally break out. Especially if we get to play the Scene soon."

He sounded so excited, I wanted to reach right through the phone and hug him. "I bet you will."

"I think so too. Did I tell you Zoe's ex-boyfriend actually works there?"

"No." He seemed to forget this was our first conversation about the fabulous Zoe. But that was okay; I got the same way sometimes when I was excited about something.

"Yeah. She's going to try to get in touch with him and set something up for us. We're so psyched!"

"I can tell," I said with a laugh. "That's great, Trev, seriously. You guys have been working really hard for a really long time. It's cool things are happening for you."

"Yeah. It's lucky for us Zoe's old band just broke up. She really fits in already."

"Uh-huh." I didn't bother to point out he'd already said that.

"We even started a couple of new songs today. Not done yet, but they're good so far."

"Cool." I grabbed Gordo the wonder pig and hugged him, closing my eyes and picturing Trevor playing his guitar. "I can't wait to hear your next set of demos."

"Don't worry. You'll be the first to get them! I can't wait to hear what you think of the new songs. You have great taste!"

"I know. That's why we get along so well," I said with a laugh.

He laughed too. "True."

There was a pause, and I opened my mouth to tell him about Kaz's party. Before I got a word out, though, he spoke up again.

"Anyway, it's great talking to you, but I should probably go."

"What?" I blurted out, sitting up straight.

"Sorry, Chloe," he said. "I'm beat, and we're meeting again tomorrow morning to work on those new songs some more."

"Oh," I murmured. So much for that late-night chat I'd been looking forward to. It felt as if we'd barely started talking! I still wanted to tell him about Kaz's party, and fill him in on the latest preparations for the dance marathon, and maybe even talk him into a little sing-along like we did sometimes. . . .

But I supposed it could wait. What good was telling him all that if he fell asleep halfway through?

"Okay, sweet dreams," I said, trying to hide my disappointment. "I'll text you tomorrow."

"Cool. Night, night, Chloe."

I set my phone aside, still smiling at his obvious excitement. He was so talented, so devoted to his music. He deserved to make it big if anyone did.

And I'll be right there supporting him, I reminded myself.

I could picture it now—Trevor up onstage with the band, screaming fans going crazy out in the audience. But I'd have the best view in the house from where I got to hang out backstage. After the show, Trevor would rush offstage and hug me, all sweaty and excited from yet another spectacular performance. We'd go eat somewhere out of the way, like Aesop's, where people were less likely to recognize him and pester him for autographs. We'd order—maybe we'd even play the menu game like my friends and I did—and talk late into the night over greasy food and coffee, then step out into the darkness where he'd grab me for a super-romantic kiss until the paparazzi spotted us and we had to run away, laughing and holding hands. . . .

It was still early, but I climbed into bed, pulled the sheet up to my chin, and hugged Gordo the wonder pig to my chest, letting that glittering future fill my mind. My eyes drifted shut, and moments later I was drifting off to sleep, already dreaming of my bright and romantic life with the coolest guy ever.

Chapter Seven

The next planning meeting for the dance marathon took place at the community center. Since it was pretty close to my house, I walked instead of catching a ride with my friends. Both Kaz and Vanessa were already there when I came in, along with Maya, almost the entire cheerleading squad, and at least two dozen people from the band, orchestra, and chorus. We were in the biggest meeting room, a cavernous space almost as large as the auditorium that doubled as an indoor basketball court in the winter. Folding chairs were set up in a semicircle at one end, and a podium stood at the center where Maya was standing.

"Good, you're here." Maya glanced at me briefly, sounding distracted as she shuffled through a bunch of papers. "We were about to get started."

"Sorry I'm late," I said. "My family went out for brunch and my parents took forever to eat. I mean, how long can you dither over whether to order the southwestern omelet or the Mediterranean one? Not to mention having to salt every bite of it separately. Seriously, my dad has a problem, you know?"

Knowing I was babbling, I shot a sidelong glance toward my friends. Vanessa smiled at me, and Kaz waved me over, indicating a free seat with them. While I was talking to Trevor the night before, I'd managed to almost forget about what Kaz had asked me at the party. But it had come roaring back as soon as I'd opened my eyes that morning. What was I going to tell him? I didn't want to break his heart or make things weird between us. But talking to Trevor had only reminded me what true romance was supposed to be all about.

"Hi," I said as I joined them, wondering if this was going to be totally uncomfortable. "Um, what's up? What's happening? What's the deal?"

"Not much, awkward girl," Kaz said, grinning. "You can relax, okay? I'm not going to bug you about you-know-what." He shot a look around at the other attendees, none of whom were paying us the slightest bit of attention. "Not the time or the venue."

"Oh. Um, good." I smiled at him, relieved. At least I had a little more time to come up with the right words.

When he turned away, Vanessa raised her eyebrows at me. I made a face at her. That was all the pantomimed conversation we had time for, since Maya called the meeting to order a second later.

"Let's start by talking about who's going to do what over the next seven days," she said. "This is going to be a ton of work if we want it to be a success."

"And we totally do," one of the other cheerleaders piped in. "Right, guys?"

I hooted and whistled along with everybody else. Kaz stood up and pumped his fist. "Let's do it!" he cried.

We all laughed and cheered again. Kaz really knows how to energize a crowd—he's always been like that. His natural enthusiasm is totally infectious. I smiled fondly as he flopped down into his chair again.

"Cool, so let's get started." Maya swept a stray strand of black hair behind her ear. Then she consulted the notebook she was holding. "Okay, so the most important part of all this is to keep on getting lots of people to pledge money to sponsor us and the kids."

One of the cheerleaders raised her hand. "Will people only be sponsoring the dancers? Or the musicians, too?"

"Both, right?" Kaz said. "I mean, the more the merrier."

I nodded. "My parents already said they're going to sponsor me and Kaz and Van and a few of the kids." I grinned. "Actually, it's more like I told them they were, and they didn't say no."

Maya chuckled. "Good. And yeah, the musicians should definitely be getting sponsors too." She scribbled something in her notebook. "But we shouldn't just settle for hitting up our friends and families, right?"

"I already asked my neighbor to sponsor me," a girl in the back called out.

"Great," Maya said. "But I was thinking even bigger than that. What if we set up a table at, like, the supermarket or wherever? We could try to get sponsors that way, too."

"Ooh, I like!" Kaz exclaimed. "They let us have the student council bake sale outside the store last year. I can ask them if we can set up a table there this week."

I smiled again. That was Kaz for you—always the first to volunteer. He really was a great guy. . . .

"I live near the store," a beefy trombone player put in. "We can use my dad's card table."

"I have photos of some of the S&D kids on my phone," Vanessa added. "I could make up a flyer with some of them so people can see where their money is going."

"Perfect. Thanks, all of you." Maya made another note and then pulled a page out of her notebook and stepped toward us. "Also, Vanessa, can you make a sign-up sheet right now? We'll pass it around and you all can sign up for shifts at the table."

"Sure." Vanessa took the sheet of paper and pen Maya handed her, and went to work.

The meeting continued from there, but my attention drifted a little. I was watching Kaz out of the corner of my eye. Yes, he was a great guy—one of the coolest people I'd ever met, actually. Any girl would be proud to have him as her boyfriend.

So why was I so convinced he wasn't the right boyfriend for

me? Somehow I'd just never seen him that way. There had to be a reason for that, right? An explanation for why Kaz inspired the term *friendship* rather than *romance*?

As usual, even thinking the word *romance* started my favorite song playing in my head. The familiar lyrics seemed to take on deeper meaning given my current thoughts. They were all about destiny, about how when you met Mr. or Ms. Right, it hit you like a bolt of lightning—leaving no doubt it was meant to be.

Nothing like that had ever happened between me and Kaz. I mean, I had no actual memory of when we'd first met, given we'd both been drooling and wearing diapers at the time. Not exactly that magical, eyes-meeting-across-a-crowded-room capital-*M* Moment, right?

So maybe that answered the question. Kaz and I were friends—best friends. Just like me and Vanessa. The kind of friends who went out on double or triple dates together and were best man or woman at each other's weddings and whose kids played together someday. Kaz would always be in my life. We definitely didn't need to involve any romance for that to be certain.

Especially since I already had my dream true romance—Trevor. Talk about a cute how-we-got-together story to tell at the wedding! I could picture it now. Kaz could do the toast and turn the whole thing into an adorable and humorous and totally romantic story. Then he and Vanessa and all the other guests would toast us as Trevor and I had our first dance together to Of Note's version of "True Romance."

The song swelled in my mind, the part toward the end when the lead singer is sort of wailing out some random vocal runs while the other guys are in the background singing,

Meant to be,
You and me.
Yeah, meant to be,
Just you and meeee . . .

I sighed, so overwhelmed by the perfection of it all that I could hardly stand it. Not that I was actually ready to propose anytime soon, or expecting him to, of course. I mean, we were only fifteen—we had plenty of time for that stuff. But for now? Yeah, it was a sweet daydream. One that reminded me how perfect this was. How Trevor and I were meant to be.

I jolted back to reality when Kaz accidentally elbowed me in the shoulder while jumping excitedly to his feet. "I have an old electric keyboard I could bring if anyone wants to play that," he called out.

Rubbing my shoulder, I blinked and glanced around, realizing I'd completely lost track of the meeting. "What are we talking about?" I whispered to Vanessa.

"Kaz had an idea for the band," Vanessa murmured back. "He thought we should branch out—make it more like a real jam band than a school band. We're figuring out who should play what extra instruments."

“Oh.” I listened as a violinist from the orchestra volunteered to play Kaz’s keyboard, and one of the percussionists said he could bring his electric guitar. More people spoke up, offering extra instruments from banjos to bongos to bass guitars. One of the cheerleaders even said her mom had an old harp she could bring in.

“I have no idea how to play it,” she said with a shrug. “But maybe someone could figure it out.”

“Kaz?” several people said at once.

He grinned. “Sure, I’ll give it a try.”

I laughed. “This is going to be the craziest band ever!” I exclaimed.

Kaz turned to smile at me. “Yeah,” he said. “It’s going to be epic!”

Maya kept us busy for another hour or so. Finally even she seemed satisfied everything was under control. “Make sure you’ve all signed up for a turn at the grocery store,” she said. “I’ll send out a group e-mail as soon as Kaz gets permission to make it official.”

“Is there any doubt?” a saxophone player called out. “The Kaz-man will get ’er done.”

“Count on it!” Toni added.

Maya smiled and checked her watch. “Anyway, I guess we’re done here for today. We’ll meet again Wednesday after school.”

Everyone started standing and stretching and chattering about the meeting and other stuff. Kaz hopped to his feet.

"Aesop's, anyone?" he suggested.

"Can't," Vanessa said. "I told my mom I'd come home right after the meeting to watch my little sister while she runs some errands."

Uh-oh. Kaz was already turning to look at me. Normally hanging out at Aesop's just the two of us wouldn't be a big deal. We'd done it a million times when Vanessa couldn't join us for some reason.

But today? Awkward City. "I should probably get home too, actually," I said quickly. "Dad said something about cleaning out the garage, and I want to make sure he isn't throwing away all my stuff."

"Oh." Kaz shrugged. "Okay. Guess I'll head over to the grocery store and see if I can talk to someone about the fund-raiser."

"Good idea," Vanessa said. "We want to make sure as many people as possible know about it."

As the three of us headed toward the exit, Kaz glanced over at me. "So, Chloe," he said, his voice a little too casual. "Not to be pushy. But, uh, have you given any thought to what I asked you yesterday?"

I tried not to let my panic show on my face. I'd pretty much reached the conclusion that Kaz and I should keep our friendship strictly . . . well, friendly. Which meant we shouldn't go to the dance together—at least not in the way he meant. But how could I just blurt that out to him right here, right now? I should at least pretend to think about it a little more, right?

"Um, I thought this wasn't the venue?" I joked weakly.

He held open the door, ushering me and Vanessa through.

"There," he said, stepping outside behind us. "Venue changed."

Vanessa chuckled, and I sighed. "I don't know, Kaz. I mean, I've been thinking about it, but it's just, you know, I'm not sure if . . ."

"It's okay," he said quickly. "Sorry. I shouldn't have pushed. I know I took you by surprise, and the least I can do is give you however much time you need." He shrugged. "I mean, the dance is still almost two weeks away, right? Plenty of time!"

"Yeah," I said.

He patted me on the arm. "Let's talk about something else," he said. "Like the marathon. Think we call pull together all those different instruments in time? Maybe we should call a rehearsal beforehand."

Vanessa's eyes lit up. "That would be fun."

"No way." Doing my best to push aside my confusing feelings about the whole dance situation, I grinned at my two best friends. "It'll be more fun if we go into it cold. Exciting, right? Anything can happen!"

They both laughed and agreed. And just like that, we were off and running, chatting easily just like we always did. I sneaked a peek over at Kaz, relieved and a little impressed with how cool he was being about this. I only hoped I could figure out a way to let him down easy—and soon. It wasn't fair to leave him hanging any longer than I had to.

After dinner that night I was in my room, the door closed and one of Of Note's songs playing softly in the background. I was trying to focus on my homework, but my mind kept drifting back to Kaz. How could I explain the different ways I felt about him and Trevor? As I pondered that, I flipped idly through some of the photos on my phone. I paused, smiling at one Trevor had sent me of him with his bandmates. He was holding his guitar with one hand, the other arm slung over the shoulders of the drummer who'd moved to Puerto Rico. The rest of the band was there too, but I hardly saw them, focusing only on Trevor. He was so handsome, so cool—the perfect boyfriend, really.

I flipped back through more photos he'd sent me of himself. He'd even dug up an old one of the two of us together at camp. Sweet, right?

After I'd looked at every picture I had of Trevor, I scrolled through the rest of the shots on my phone. Most of them were of Kaz and Vanessa, of course. I paused on one from last Halloween.

We'd been studying the Roaring Twenties in history class around that time, and the three of us had decided to dress up like that for Maya's annual costume party. Van and I had worn flapper dresses and tons of long strings of pearls, while Kaz had found a baggy striped suit and old fedora in a secondhand store. We'd posed for pictures at Vanessa's house before heading off to the party, and in this particular one Kaz was dipping me while Vanessa stood beside us, twirling her pearls. I still remembered that moment—we'd all been pretending to do the Charleston, which Kaz had looked up online and taught us. Suddenly he'd grabbed me and twirled me around, then dipped me before I caught my breath. As a result, my upside-down mouth was open in a little O, which looked perfect for the theme.

I touched the screen to make the photo larger, studying Kaz's expression. He was smiling as he looked down at me, his dark eyes filled with joy. Why had he grabbed me to dip instead of Vanessa? Was it just because I was shorter and thus easier to dip, or was it possible he'd been thinking of me differently even back then? It was a strange thought.

"What would it be like if he'd asked me out back then?" I murmured, touching the screen again to scroll to the next photo, this one showing all three of us back at it, trying to do the Charleston. "Me and Kaz . . ."

After all, if he'd asked me then, before Trevor was in the picture, I might have said yes. I tried to imagine it—actually going out with him, being his girlfriend.

But it was just too weird. Besides, it wasn't last year—it was now. Going to the dance as Kaz's date would mean leaving Vanessa on her own, since she still refused to let me set her up with anyone.

And what about Trevor? If I said yes to Kaz, would I have to "break up" with Trevor, even though we weren't even officially going out?

I sighed, wishing Kaz had never asked me out. That way, I wouldn't have to worry our friendship was going to change. . . .

Still, as I scrolled to yet another photo, this one showing the three of us standing together with our arms around one another, grinning like fools, I couldn't quite stop myself from trying to picture it. Me and Kaz walking into the dance together. Putting my arms around him for the first slow song, maybe resting my head on his shoulder . . .

Suddenly I heard a loud squawk from somewhere outside. Glancing toward the window, I set my phone aside.

"What was that?" I muttered.

Another squawk rang out, and then something that sounded more like a musical note. Then another, and another—after a few more notes, I recognized the first line of a Sousa march we'd played in band recently.

"Oh man," I said.

Hurrying over, I looked out the window. Kaz was down in my yard, oboe at his lips. He was swaying and tapping his foot as he played the march's snappy melody.

I laughed and then yanked open the window. Kaz heard me and stopped playing, squinting up at me.

"Oh, hi," he said, as if it were the most natural thing in the world for him to be standing in my mom's petunias playing Sousa. Which, for him, maybe it was.

"What are you doing out there, you nut?" I exclaimed.

He grinned and held up his oboe. "I'm serenading you," he said. "That's supposed to be romantic, right? Like in the song?"

I realized he was talking about "True Romance." There was a line in there about music being the language of the soul, and serenading each other and stuff. Whoa. Maybe I'd waited too long to let him down easy.

"Wait right there," I told him. "I'm coming out."

Moments later I burst out into the front yard. Kaz was waiting, looking pleased with himself.

"What do you think?" he asked. "Pretty romantic, right?"

"Yeah, I guess," I replied with another laugh. "It might be more romantic if you'd chosen a different song, though."

"Oh." He looked at his oboe. "Right."

"But it's still pretty romantic," I added hurriedly. "Thanks."

Instead of answering, he raised the oboe to his lips and tootled out the melody to "You Are My Sunshine."

"Better?" he asked when he'd finished.

"A little," I said.

"Hold on . . ." Once again, he lifted his instrument. This time he played "I Could Have Danced All Night" from *My Fair Lady*. Oh wow. We'd done that show at summer arts camp a few years back, and I'd hummed that song constantly for the next six months. Of course Kaz would remember, even though I'd pretty much forgotten it myself until that moment.

"That's more like it," I admitted after he'd ended with a flourish.

His grin was back. "Good. You're so into true romance and stuff lately, I figured I'd give you something to think about—you know, while you make up your mind." With a quick salute, he turned and hurried off.

"Wait! Where are you going?" I called, taking a few steps after him.

But it was too late. He'd already disappeared into the darkness.

I stood there staring after him for a moment, wondering what to do. Kaz was so sweet. He definitely wasn't making it easy for me to stick with my plan to keep him in the friend zone.

Realizing I was shivering out there in only my T-shirt and sweats, I hurried back inside, shaking off the evening chill. Back upstairs, I wandered over to my desk and picked up my phone, pulling up that photo of Kaz dipping me. When had things changed between us? And why hadn't I noticed until Kaz had said something?

And more important, what was I supposed to do about it? He was trying so hard—maybe it wouldn't be so bad to say yes to his invitation. To go to the dance together and see how it went. What was the worst thing that could happen? I mean, there was Trevor. But he was far away, and Kaz was right here being his sweet, goofy, lovable self. That had to count for something, right?

I picked up my phone, tempted to call Kaz right then and tell him his serenade had swept me off my feet. Tell him I'd be his date for the dance.

Then the phone rang in my hand, making me jump. For half a second I was sure it was Kaz calling for my answer.

But no—my rational mind took over quickly. The ringtone wasn't the Twilight Zone theme; it was a guitar riff. Trevor.

I bit my lip, staring at the name on the screen. For a second I was tempted to decline the call and text Trevor later to apologize for missing his call. Because I needed to think about this thing with Kaz; I needed to decide what to do.

But that wouldn't be nice. At the very least I should answer and tell Trevor I couldn't talk right now.

"Hello?" I said into the phone. "Trevor? Listen, I—"

He didn't let me finish. "Guess what." he said. "I'm coming after all!"

"Huh?" I blinked, confused. "Coming where?"

"There. To my relatives' place, I mean. The reunion is on again!"

Chapter Eight

I was so stunned, I couldn't respond for a second. I just sat there, my mouth opening and closing like I was some kind of demented fish gasping for air.

"Chloe?" Trevor said after a moment. "Are you still there?"

"Wh-when are you coming?" I blurted out, still trying to catch up.

"We're making a whole vacation of it," he said. "My stepdad says he's not driving that far just to turn around and come home again after a couple of days."

He sounded slightly disgruntled, but I ignored that. "When?" I said again.

"This Friday. We'll be there through the following weekend. Are you going to be around? Because seeing you is pretty much the only silver lining to missing over a week's worth of rehearsals." He sighed. "I tried to tell my mom I need to be here now, with the new drummer and all, but it's like I'm speaking a whole other language or something—"

"Hold on," I cut him off. My mind had finally clicked into gear, calculating what he'd just told me. "Wait! But that means . . ." I gasped. "Oh my gosh, this is so incredible! My school's having a dance, and I was already sort of daydreaming earlier about if you were here and we could go, and thinking about whether some stuff is meant to be, and . . ." Realizing I was babbling and probably not making much sense to him, I forced myself to stop and take a deep breath. "Trevor," I said. "Will you go to the dance with me?"

He laughed. "Are you serious? You've got a school dance coming up? While I'm in town?"

"Uh-huh. It's a week from Saturday night. So what do you say?" I held my breath.

He didn't keep me in suspense. "Absolutely," he said. "I'd love to go!"

I let out the breath and smiled. "Cool," I said. "I can't wait for you to meet everyone. That'll be the perfect time." Then I remembered something else. "Oh!" I exclaimed. "Unless . . . Did you say you're getting here this coming weekend?"

"Uh-huh. We're driving down on Friday after my stepdad gets off work."

"But that means you can come to the dance marathon, too!" I

exclaimed, hardly believing how great this was turning out. "It's this coming Sunday."

"The what? Another dance?"

"No, the dance marathon. It's that fund-raiser I told you about, the one for the kids?" I was getting more excited by the second. "I'm playing in the band, and the cheerleaders and some of the kids are going to dance—remember?"

"Sure, yeah," he said. "I didn't realize it was so soon."

"It's going to be superfun." I gasped as another thought popped into my mind. "Hey, maybe you can even play with us! It would be cool to have more guitarists—especially a great one like you."

"Oh okay." He sounded kind of pleased by the compliment. "Could be fun, I guess. But I'll have to let you know, okay? I'm not sure yet what's happening with the whole reunion deal."

I wanted to argue, to tell him he had to come to the marathon. I mean, how could he possibly miss out on something like that when he was only a few towns away? It was the perfect chance for us to spend the entire day together.

But I bit my tongue. He knew all that; he was going to try to work it out but didn't want to make any promises he couldn't keep. Family first, right? I could only imagine what my own parents would say if I wanted to skip out on some big family reunion to hang out with my boyfriend. Not that our family reunions were a big deal, since we pretty much all lived within half an hour from one another. Still.

"Okay, sure," I said. "Let me know when you find out."

"Will do. I can probably work it out," he said. "Anyway, it's going to be so weird being back in my old stomping grounds, you know? I haven't been back in a couple of years."

"Yeah." I tried to imagine that. I'd lived in the same town—the same house—for my entire life. "I can't believe I'm finally going to see you in person again after all this time!"

"Hope you won't be disappointed." His voice took on a teasing tone.

"We'll see," I teased back. "I hope you haven't been sending me some cute guy's pictures all this time."

He laughed. "Uh-oh—busted!"

My bedroom door slammed open, and my brother stuck his head in. "Mom says it's time for lights out," he announced loudly.

"Hey," I said. "Did you ever hear of knocking?"

"Who's that?" Trevor asked.

"My rude little brother." I made an ugly face at Timothy. He responded with an obnoxious gesture and then slammed the door shut again. "But I guess I need to go. I don't want to annoy my parents so they ground me or something—I want to be free as a bird to spend tons of time with you while you're here!"

"Cool." He chuckled. "Okay, guess I should hit the sack too. The guys and I—um, I mean the band, you know—will have to pack in as many rehearsals as we can before I leave on Friday. Zoe still thinks she can get us in at the club soon, and we need to be ready."

"You will be. You guys are supertalented, and that's the main thing, right?"

"I guess." He didn't sound too certain.

But I wasn't really focused on his band just then. I couldn't believe I was going to see him in less than a week! "I'll text you tomorrow so we can start making plans and stuff, okay?"

"Sure," he said. "Talk to you then. Good night, Chloe."

As soon as I hung up, I immediately called Vanessa. When she picked up, I didn't bother to say hello. "Oh my gosh, you're not going to believe this. . . ." I began, barely pausing for breath as I filled her in.

She was almost as excited as I was. At first all she could manage were some squeals and chirps and other noises. Finally she said, gasping, "This could totally be another verse!"

I knew what she meant without asking, and started to sing the chorus of our favorite song: "*True romance, it's the air that we breathe. Just us two together. Yeah, just you and me.*"

About two words into it, Vanessa joined in. We sang it twice, and then I collapsed onto my bed with a sigh, resting my head on Gordo's soft pink belly.

"I can't believe this is happening!" I exclaimed. "It's seriously like a dream come true. A daydream, at least."

"I know, right?" Vanessa sounded wistful. "I hope I meet a guy as cool as Trevor someday."

"You will. I still want to find you your own romantic date for the dance, remember? Now we can double!"

"Don't bother," she said. "Since you'll be with Trevor now, I might as well just go stag with Kaz."

Kaz. I gulped, realizing I'd sort of forgotten him when I'd heard Trevor's news. My gaze wandered to the window, where I'd looked out on my geeky troubadour just a few minutes earlier.

"Right," I said. "Listen, I haven't told Kaz about Trevor's visit yet. I'll have to let him down easy, I guess."

"Oh." She sounded troubled. "Right."

"Don't say anything to him until I have a chance to talk to him, okay?"

"I won't. Are you going to call him now?"

I closed my eyes, not looking forward to this. How was I going to give him my news without breaking his heart? The tune from "I Could Have Danced All Night" whispered through my mind, and I sighed. "I'm not sure this is something I should tell him on the phone," I told Vanessa. "Besides, it's getting late. I'll talk to him in the morning."

Mr. Graves had scheduled band rehearsal on Monday morning before school. We had extra morning rehearsals at least once a week, and more often before a big concert or whatever.

When I walked into the band room, Vanessa was nowhere in sight. Kaz was there, though. He was goofing around with the percussionists at the back of the room. I dropped my clarinet case on my seat and headed that way, arriving just in time to witness Kaz playing a fast-paced jungle rhythm on the timpani with his oboe.

"Don't let Mr. G catch you doing that," I said with a faint smile. "You know how he feels about respecting your instrument." I cleared my throat, casting a sidelong look at the percussionists. I definitely didn't want to do this in front of them. "Um, can I talk to you?"

"Isn't that what you're doing?" said one of the other guys, grinning.

"Yeah," another percussionist said. "That's what Chloe's always doing—talking."

The only female percussionist rolled her eyes. "Look who's talking, Dave," she said.

Kaz laughed. But I guess he must have seen something in my face, because he didn't join in on the joking. "Later, guys," he said, following me away.

Ignoring the hoots and razzing comments drifting after us, I led the way to a quiet corner behind the acoustical shell. Then I turned to face Kaz. This wasn't going to be easy, but I knew I had to be straight with him and not leave him hanging. He'd do the same for me—I was sure of that.

"Well?" he said hopefully. "Does this mean you finally have an answer for me?" He grinned. "Just kidding—it hasn't been *that* long."

I lowered my gaze to his chin, not wanting to see the eager look in those familiar brown eyes. "Yeah. The thing is, I just found out that, um, Trevor is coming to town."

"Oh." He looked confused for a second. "Um, that's nice, I guess?"

"Yeah. As it happens, he'll be here the weekend of the dance."

Kaz isn't stupid. He knitted his brow for a second, but then understanding dawned quickly.

"Oh," he said, his voice quiet and a little sad now. "I see."

I chewed my lower lip. "I'm sorry, Kaz. I thought about it, I really did. Especially after that romantic serenade last night." I couldn't help a half smile at the memory. "That was really sweet. But don't you think we're better off as friends? I mean, I'd hate to mess that up, you know?"

"Yeah." He wasn't quite meeting my eyes anymore, instead staring down at the oboe he was holding. Kaz doesn't show every emotion in full Technicolor the way Vanessa does, but he's not exactly Mr. Poker Face, either. I could tell he was disappointed.

"Are you okay?" I said, touching his arm. "I mean, we're okay, right? This isn't going to be weird?"

"Definitely not." He finally met my gaze with a smile, though it looked sort of forced. "We're totally fine. Friends forever, right?"

"Totally." I was relieved but still a little worried. "You'll go to the dance though, right? Van's counting on you—Oh! That gives me a great idea." I brightened as a brilliant thought struck me. "Why don't you two go together?"

He looked confused again. "Don't we always? I mean, usually you're there too, but—"

"No, I mean you two could go as, like, a real date." The more I thought about it, the better I liked this. I was a genius! Kaz was too good for the general public. If I wasn't available, that left only my other best friend good enough for him. "Seriously, Kaz, at least think about it, okay? You should definitely ask her! Who knows, maybe that's how this was meant to turn out all along! It'd be like fate, right? You and Van, me and Trev . . ."

"I guess," Kaz said uncertainly. "I'll think about it. Just give me a chance to recover from my heartbreak first, okay?"

He clutched his chest in the general vicinity of his heart. I could tell he was going for a joking tone, but his face didn't quite hold up its end of the deal. His eyes still looked kind of forlorn in a way that made my stomach clench.

Mr. Graves came into the room and called for order, so we hurried back to our seats. As I quickly put together my clarinet and warmed up, I kept sneaking peeks at Kaz, who was playing the oboe today and thus sitting just a few yards away. He was smiling and chatting with the girl who played bassoon, looking perfectly normal. Well, okay, almost normal. Was it my imagination, or did his eyes still look sad?

Don't flatter yourself, girl, I chided myself. He'll get over it.

I was sure that was true. But I still wasn't happy at the thought that I'd hurt him, even temporarily. What else could I do, though? Okay, so maybe for a few brief moments I'd actually entertained the thought of what might happen if Kaz and I got together. But that had just been a daydream, a passing what-if.

Because Trevor was my dream guy, and now he was coming to town just in time for the dance. That had to be a sign. Right?

Right, I told myself firmly. Resting my clarinet in the crook of my arm, I pulled out my phone and brought up that photo of Trevor playing his guitar. Just to remind myself what true romance really looked like.

Chapter Nine

Glancing at the front of the classroom, I saw Ms. Batra still had her back to the students as she scribbled factoids about the industrial revolution all over the board. I carefully slid my phone out from under my leg, ignoring the knowing smirk of the kid across the aisle.

Trevor had texted me earlier, but I hadn't dared text him back during English class. Mr. Ortiz had a habit of confiscating phones when he caught anyone using one. And I had way too much planning to do to lose my phone this week. It was already Tuesday, and Trevor and I had been texting back and forth pretty much nonstop since the big news. He still wasn't sure exactly what his family had planned, but he'd already contacted his seventeen-year-old cousin and found out he had a girlfriend in my town and was more than happy to let Trevor tag along when he visited her—including the night of the dance.

What were the odds, right? But I was getting used to the way fate or destiny or true romance or whatever was pushing us together. Trevor and I were definitely meant to be, and I liked the feeling. Smiling at the thought, I scanned his last text and then started one of my own.

I was thinking we could meet for pizza when u get here on Fri night, since I know that's your fave. There's a really good place here in town. What do u think?

Checking the front of the room again, I could tell Ms. Batra was almost finished with her scribbles. I tucked my phone out of sight beneath my leg again, not really expecting to hear back from Trevor right away.

To my surprise, however, it vibrated just a few moments later. Sliding it out just enough to read, I saw his response.

Pizza sounds great. I'll ask Jon if he can bring me over then. It's probably fine since he usually goes out with his gf on Friday nights. Will let u know later for sure. Can't wait to see u!

"Chloe?" The teacher's sharp voice brought my head up with a snap. "Are you taking a nap, or would you like to start us off by reading chapter twelve to the class?"

"Um, sure." Quickly nudging my phone back out of sight, I cleared my throat and started to read, doing my best not to grin like an idiot and give myself away.

• • •

At lunch I tossed my brown bag onto the table and slid into my seat across from Vanessa. She was already tearing into her sandwich. The girl might be skinny, but she eats like a horse.

"Hear from Trev?" she mumbled through a mouthful of half-chewed ham and cheese.

"He's in for Friday night pizza." I beamed at her. "Our first real date!"

She swallowed and smiled, raising her hand for a fist bump. "That's amazing," she said. "So romantic!"

"Yeah, kind of," I said. "Although having our first real date be the dance—or, you know, some candlelit dinner or something—would be more romantic than pizza at Angelo's, you know? Maybe I should think of Friday as just being, like, two old friends meeting up for pizza."

"Maybe." She shrugged. "I guess the song doesn't say anything about pepperoni, right?"

I laughed. "No. But the dance will definitely count as a date! Even the song says so—dancing in the moonlight, right?"

She hummed a few bars and then reached for her water bottle. "You guys are going to get together between this Friday and next Saturday, though, right? Is he coming to the marathon?"

My smile faded slightly. "He's not sure yet. He's trying to find out when all his reunion stuff is supposed to be." I opened my bag and dumped out my lunch. "I guess his family's a little scatterbrained when it comes to that stuff."

Vanessa sipped her water. "I hope he comes, because I don't

think I can wait a whole week to get a look at this guy in person." She giggled. "Kaz and I might have to put on disguises and come spy on you two at the pizza place."

"Yeah, funny."

I shot a look toward the cafeteria line. Kaz would be emerging from there any second now. I still felt funny talking too much about Trevor in front of Kaz, even though I was pretty sure his crush on me would fade quickly now that he knew I wasn't into him that way.

But maybe I could hurry that along? "By the way, speaking of Kaz," I said. "Are you two going to the dance together or what?"

"Sure, I guess." Vanessa grabbed one of my carrot sticks. "Don't we always?"

"No, not like that." I gave her a meaningful look. "I was thinking you two should go as, like, a date. You know? That way we could double."

Vanessa looked surprised. "Oh. Um, I don't know. It seems weird to think of Kaz that way, you know?"

"Welcome to my world." I picked up a carrot and stared at it. "Think about it though, okay? It would make me feel a lot better about rejecting him if I knew there was a chance he'd ended up on a dream date with someone even better."

She blushed. "I don't know about that. . . ."

Just then my phone vibrated. I usually kept the ringer off during school, even during the times, like lunch, when we were allowed to use our phones. Otherwise, I tended to forget to switch it off again.

It was Trevor: *FYI, found out the big reunion picnic is the second Saturday of the visit.*

For a second my heart completely stopped beating. I swear it did.

"No," I said aloud. "But that's the day of the dance!"

"Huh?" Vanessa looked up from her food.

I was already furiously typing out my response: *The second Sat is the dance! Does this mean u can't go?!?!?!?*

While I waited for his response, I showed Vanessa both texts. I was too worked up to speak, but luckily, she got it right away. Her eyes widened, and she wordlessly offered me one of her mom's homemade lemon squares. But I waved it away, suddenly too queasy to eat.

Fortunately, Trevor didn't keep me in suspense for long.

No, sorry, don't freak out, lol! The picnic is during the day. My cousin Jon is def planning to cut out in plenty of time to get us both to your dance. I'm sure we will both be totally fed up with our fam by then and ready to escape, lol!!!

I practically melted with relief. "Oh man," I muttered, flashing the phone at Vanessa so she could see. Then I texted back.

Good!!!! U had me worried there for a sec, lol!

He texted back almost immediately: *Sorry, sorry! U know I would never miss the big dance! Can't wait to dance in the moonlight with u!!!* ☺

I sighed. "He's so sweet," I murmured, feeling a flush of happiness wash over me. Who could have predicted, back at that kids' music camp all those years ago, we'd end up here? Talk about a romantic story worthy of a song! Maybe Trevor would write one about us someday. I made a mental note to drop some hints while he was here. Who knew? Maybe our romance would even lead to Of Note's first big hit!

Then I spotted Kaz heading toward us, tray in hand. With one more glance at Trevor's last text, I shoved my phone away out of sight.

Chapter Ten

By Friday afternoon I was so excited, I couldn't stand it. I spent all of last period staring at the clock on the wall, willing the hands to move faster. Luckily, Ms. Farley didn't notice. Vanessa, however, did. When the bell finally rang, she fell into step beside me as I bolted from the room.

"Don't worry," she said with a smile. "You can borrow my notes from today. Because you looked like you were a million miles away all period. And not thinking about biology at all." She giggled. "Unless it was *Trevor's* biology. Or maybe chemistry?" She waggled her eyebrows at me.

"Clever." I grinned. "Anyway, can you blame me? I mean, I'll actually be face-to-face with Trevor in"—I checked my watch—"two hours and twenty-seven minutes. Not that I'm counting."

She laughed. "Okay, so let's go get you all cute."

"Hey," Kaz said breathlessly, catching up to us. "You guys took off so fast, you practically left skid marks on the floor! Let me guess—you're craving random menu items from Aesop's?" He grinned at us hopefully.

"Oh." I shot a look at Vanessa. "Um, sorry, no time for Aesop's today. Trevor's coming, remember?"

"Oh right. Mr. True Romance." His expression went sort of blank.

I wasn't sure what that meant. Was he still upset about the dance thing?

Doubtful, I told myself. He was probably just trying to think up a funny insult to make about Trevor, as usual.

"I've got to hit my locker," Vanessa told me. "Meet you out front in five?"

"Yeah." As she hurried off, I looked at Kaz again, a twinge of guilt and concern making me want to take action. "Hey," I said. "Speaking of romance, have you given any thought to asking Van to the dance? You two would make an awfully cute couple."

"Hmm." Kaz shrugged. "We are both fine-looking specimens. I'll give you that."

"Modest too," I said with a laugh. "Just think about it, okay?"

Vanessa and I had a great time getting ready. I was a pretty fine-looking specimen myself by the time I hugged her good-bye at my front door.

"Wish me luck," I said.

She squeezed me. "You won't need it. Trevor is going to die when he sees you!"

"Let's hope not." I laughed and then blew her a kiss as I hurried down the front walk.

It usually takes about ten minutes to walk from my house into town, but I made it in about half that. Hurrying past Aesop's, I crossed the next street and stopped in front of Angelo's. Taking a deep breath, I realized I was nervous.

That wasn't like me. I almost never get nervous except maybe when I think I've blown a test or something. After all, I've been performing music for just about as long as I can remember, and I barely remember what stage fright even feels like.

This was different, though. This was true romance. Which meant it was perfectly normal to be nervous, right? There was even a line in the song about getting all breathless and butterflies-in-the-stomach when you first looked into your true love's eyes. . . .

Smiling as I thought about that, I pushed through Angelo's heavy glass doors. The place was crowded, but a couple of glances were enough to tell me Trevor wasn't there yet.

Checking my watch, I saw I was a little early. Good. He'd be able to walk in and see me there. Maybe our eyes would meet across the crowded room or something super True Romancey like that. . . .

"Hi, Chloe!" a cheerful voice greeted me. "What's up? You meeting Kaz and Vanessa here? I haven't seen them come in yet."

I blinked, yanking myself out of my daydreams to focus on the perky cheerleader grinning at me and holding an armful of menus. It was Toni. I'd totally forgotten she worked at Angelo's.

"Hi, Toni," I said. "Um, no, I'm actually meeting a guy here. His name's Trevor?"

She nodded, not seeming fazed by that. "Cool. Want me to seat you while you wait?"

"Sure."

She led me to one of the only free tables in the place, a two-person booth in the back. Perfect.

Well, okay, it would've been even more perfect if it were up by the windows instead of at the back kind of near the bathrooms. At least we'd have plenty of privacy.

I slid into the seat facing the door so I could keep a lookout. Toni set a couple of menus on the table.

"What's this guy look like?" she asked. "I'll send him right back when he gets here."

"Dark hair, green eyes," I said. "My age. Really cute."

"Really!" Toni looked intrigued. "But wait, aren't you and Kaz, you know . . ." She waggled her eyebrows.

I frowned. Why did the entire cheerleading squad seem to have us paired off? I figured it was probably Maya's fault, but before I could explain things to Toni, someone called out for more iced tea, so she shrugged at me apologetically and hurried off. I was kind of glad to see her go. I always get a kick out of Toni's peppiness, but she tended to ask a lot of questions, and I wasn't in the mood to be grilled about my nonromance with Kaz at the moment. Especially with Trevor due to arrive any second. Quickly, I checked my hair in the back of a spoon and tried to get into a True Romance mood.

And when I looked up again, there he was in the doorway. I would have recognized him from a mile away, let alone a few yards. He looked just like he did in his pictures, only even hotter. He was standing with a slightly older guy with long greasy hair and a pointy chin. The older guy had his arm around a girl I vaguely recognized as a senior from my school.

Toni spotted them too. She rushed over and greeted them, pointing toward my table. The older guy and the girl just glanced my way and then turned and left the pizza place. But Trevor came toward me, a tentative smile on his face. His beautiful, beautiful face. I couldn't quite believe how cute he was in person—like an honest-to-goodness rock star, for real!

When he got closer, I saw he had a guitar slung over his shoulder by a long strap. It was tucked behind his back so I hadn't noticed it at first.

"Hey," he said when he reached me. "Chloe?"

"The one and only," I replied lightly. "Steve, right?"

Trevor looked confused. "Um . . ."

"Kidding," I said quickly. Okay, maybe Trevor was going to have to readjust to my sense of humor. "Sit down?"

He did so, setting his guitar carefully in the corner of the booth first. I glanced at it.

"I didn't realize you were bringing that," I said. "You should have told me. I could've brought my clarinet, and it'd be like a double date."

He raised an eyebrow. "Kidding again, right?"

"Sort of." I grinned weakly. "I'm kind of hoping you planned to serenade me or something?"

He glanced at the guitar, frowning slightly. "Actually, I had to bring it if I wanted it to stay in one piece," he said. "My cousin's kid is a total brat, and I was afraid he'd mess with it."

"Your cousin has a kid?" I shot a look toward the doorway where his cousin had just been standing.

Trevor followed my gaze. "My other cousin," he said. "Jon's older sister. She's twenty-four, and the kid is, like, two. Maybe three?" He shrugged, still looking a little cranky. "I'm not good with kids' ages."

"Yeah, me either," I said uncertainly. So far this wasn't quite the romantic dream reunion I'd imagined. "But listen, let's start over, okay? Hi, Trevor. It's me, Chloe. You look great!"

He looked confused for a second. Then he grinned, which made his whole face light up. And all of a sudden the weird awkwardness disappeared—poof!—and my old pal Trevor from camp was standing there in front of me.

"Sorry," he said, running a hand through his hair. "It's been a long day, you know?" He leaned forward. "You look great too. Fantastic, actually. No, make that beautiful."

"Thanks." Was I turning into Vanessa? Because I was pretty

sure I actually blushed at that. "You look great too. Oh wait, I said that already, didn't I?'

He chuckled. "It's okay. It's really great to see you, Chloe. Weird, but great."

"Weird in a good way, right?" I said. "Because I know exactly what you mean."

He smiled. Our eyes met. I could have looked at him forever, but after a moment it felt a little awkward, so I grabbed a menu and handed it to him. "You hungry?"

"Starved. So what's good here?" Taking the menu, he started flipping through it.

"Everything." I still couldn't take my eyes off him. It was hard to believe the skinny, slightly geeky ten-year-old kid I'd known at camp had turned into . . . *this*.

"Cool. Meat lovers with mushrooms okay?" he said, tossing down the menu. "We could split it."

I didn't bother to tell him I didn't like mushrooms. With all the butterflies stampeding around in my stomach at the moment, I wasn't going to be able to eat much anyway.

"Sure," I said. "So, I can't believe you're here! It's like camp ended ten minutes ago, right?"

"Yeah." He grinned. "Speaking of camp, guess who just tracked me down on Facebook? Remember that kid with the runny nose and the Birkenstocks?"

I gasped. "You mean Granola Greg? Oh my gosh! How is he?"

With that, we were off and running, reminiscing about old

camp friends and memories. Somewhere in the middle of it Toni showed up to take our order, though I barely noticed. It felt so good to talk to Trevor in person—no parents coming in to tell me to turn off my phone, no distractions from band rehearsals or studying or whatever.

After a while Toni arrived again bearing our pizza. "Here you go, guys," she announced, sliding it onto the little metal stand. "I even asked the chef to give you extra mushrooms—no charge."

Great. Still, Trevor looked pleased. "Thanks, gorgeous," he said, flashing her a grin. "It looks great."

"You're welcome, beautiful," Toni responded without missing a beat.

Gorgeous, huh? Well, okay, Toni was gorgeous, so what? Trevor had already called me beautiful and fantastic and weird, and those were much more interesting compliments, right?

He reached for a slice as Toni hurried off. I did the same, trying not to wrinkle my nose as the stench of mushrooms wafted up at me. "Cheers," I said, hoisting my slice.

Trevor was about to take a bite, but then he paused, smiled, and lifted his own slice toward me. "Cheers."

We bumped slices and then each took a bite. I even managed to find a spot that didn't have any mushrooms on it—score!

"So," Trevor said. "You're still playing the clarinet, huh?" He grinned. "When are you going to take up the bass or something and join a real band?"

I rolled my eyes. "Why bother?" I joked in return. "Any band

I joined could never compete with the fabulous Of Note, right?"

"For sure." His eyes lit up. "Not to brag, but we're sounding tighter than ever since Zoe joined. She's exactly what we needed, I guess, you know?"

"Uh-huh." I nibbled carefully at the edge of my pizza. "She sounds great."

"She is. We're all already writing tons of new songs together. . . ." He continued for a while, telling me all about their latest rehearsals and big plans for the future. I listened eagerly, wanting to know everything about him. Not to mention loving his passion for his music—after all, that was what had first bonded us way back in our camp days.

Ten seconds later Trevor's phone buzzed. Actually, it only *felt* like ten seconds. It was actually probably more like an hour, given that the pizza in front of us had mostly disappeared, and there was a whole different set of customers sitting at the tables nearby.

Trevor checked his phone. "That's Jon," he said. "He's picking me up in five minutes."

"Already?" I frowned. "But you just got here! Can't you ask him for a little more time?"

"Probably not a good idea." Trevor grimaced. "He's the only one who's willing to drive me around this week so I'm not stuck at my aunt and uncle's house the entire time. I don't want to piss him off, you know?" He reached over and touched my arm, shooting me a sweet little half smile. "But this has been fun, right? It's so great to see you, Chloe."

"You too," I mumbled, still not quite believing he had to leave already. We'd barely had a chance to talk about anything except camp and his band—I had so much more to tell him, so much I wanted to ask him! And I definitely didn't want to wait until the dance next weekend to continue the magic.

I opened my mouth to ask if he was coming to the marathon on Sunday. But he spoke up again before I could.

"Maybe we can get together tomorrow night?" he said. "Jon's coming up here to go to a party with his girl, and he already said I could tag along. Maybe we could do dinner and a movie or something?"

My heart fluttered. This was more like it! I cleared my throat and started to sing: *"I knew my dreams of true romance would all come true someday. Like dinner and a movie out with my most special bae."*

He grinned. "Nice voice. If we didn't already have a lead singer"—he pointed to himself—"I'd ask you to join the band!"

I laughed. "Anyway, that's my way of saying dinner and a movie sounds perfect." I knew Vanessa was going to be excited when she heard about this. Pizza was one thing, but dinner and a movie? That definitely counted as a date!

"Great. Jon wants to be at the party by seven, so I could meet you somewhere around quarter of."

"Perfect. Can he drop you at the mall movie theater? There's a good Italian place we could walk to from there after the movie."

"Sounds like a plan." He stood up and reached for his guitar.

I leaned forward, still not quite ready for this to end. Although at least now I had another date to look forward to. Maybe even more than one. Which reminded me . . . "By the way, don't forget the dance marathon's on Sunday," I said. "Did you figure out yet if you can make it?"

"Not sure." He carefully slung his guitar over his shoulder, then turned and held out his hand.

For a second I wasn't sure why. Then I blushed as I realized he was helping me out of the booth.

Not that I needed help. I mean, I've been successfully getting myself in and out of booths for, oh, at least twelve or thirteen years now. Still, it was a pretty romantic thing to do.

I took his hand, bracing myself for the magical tingle of his touch. "Thanks," I said. "Um, so when do you think you'll know? I mean, about the marathon."

He squeezed my hand and let go once I was on my feet. "I promise I'll try to pin down my family sometime tonight if I can," he said. "I can probably let you know by the time we meet up tomorrow night."

"Oh. Right." I followed him as he headed for the door. "Okay." Tomorrow night? That didn't leave me much time to get excited if he was coming to the marathon on Sunday.

Then again I was already excited about the fund-raiser. Trevor coming would just be icing on the cake.

"I hope you can come," I said. "It should be lots of fun. The kids are a riot, and the band is going to be supercrazy. Kaz might even . . . " I gulped, suddenly realizing it was the first time I'd really mentioned Kaz. The first time I'd thought about Kaz, actually. Why did that make me feel guilty? Today was supposed to be about me and Trevor, not me and Kaz. "Um, I mean, someone's bringing a harp, and a few of us might give it a try, and . . . " I burbled, trying to cover my confused feelings. "Anyway, it'll be interesting."

Luckily, Trevor didn't seem to notice my weirdness. Once we were outside, he turned to face me. "This has been really fun, Chloe," he said with a smile. "Getting to see you again, I mean." He swung his guitar around to his front and started to strum.

I watched his long, graceful fingers dance expertly over the strings, feeling that butterfly flutter again. He hummed along for a moment, then started to sing: "Chloe, Chloe, Chloe, you're the girl for me. Chloe, Chloe, Chloe, you're the only one I see."

Wow. Just wow. For a second I was afraid I'd fallen and hit my head or something and was dreaming this. Because it was seriously too perfect, wasn't it? Was I really being serenaded by the guy of my dreams right here on the main street of my town?

Speaking of which, a few passersby paused and gave Trevor and me strange looks. I guess it's not every day you see a future rock star singing to a girl on a street corner. But I ignored them. All I cared about was soaking up this moment.

He stopped playing after a moment and smiled. "What do you think?"

"I think—I think . . ." For once, I had nothing to say. No words could express how amazing this was.

"I hope you like it," he said. "It's just a little something I've been messing with lately."

"I love it." I stepped forward, touching his arm. "Thank you. It's amazing. *You're* amazing."

He smiled back, strumming a few chords from my song, and it was like we were all alone out there on the busy street. All alone in the world.

But the spell was broken when Jon's car screeched to a stop at the curb nearby. He stuck his head out the open window.

"Yo, Trev!" he called. "Let's move."

Trevor stopped playing again. "Gotta go," he told me, reaching out and squeezing my hand. "See you tomorrow?"

"For sure." I sighed and smiled as I watched him set his guitar in the back and then climb into the passenger seat, not taking my eyes off Jon's car until it disappeared around the corner.

Then I turned and headed for home, already looking forward to tomorrow night.

Chapter Eleven

My friends and I spent Saturday morning setting up for the dance marathon, turning the smelly school gym into a magical dance party wonderland—or at least making it look a little less boring and gross.

Afterward we went to Aesop's. "I hope I get a chance to bring Trevor here this week," I said as we walked in. As soon as the words were out of my mouth, I felt a twinge of guilt. I was trying not to talk about Trevor too much in front of Kaz in case he was still feeling bummed about how things had worked out.

"Yeah, right." He didn't sound bummed at all as he led the way to our usual booth. "We still haven't seen this guy, you know. Are you sure you're not going to show up at the dance next week with that stuffed pig of yours in a tux?"

I laughed, stepping forward to take my usual spot beside Vanessa. But Kaz beat me to it, sliding in beside her.

"Hey," I said. "You took my seat."

"Actually, I thought I should sit by Van today," Kaz said.

Vanessa blushed. "I was just getting ready to tell you, Chloe," she said. "Kaz and I decided, um . . ."

"We're taking your advice," Kaz took over. "Giving this dating thing a try. Starting with the dance."

"Oh!" I was so startled, I almost knocked over the water glass as I slid in across from them, though I tried to cover it up by grabbing the glass and gulping down about half of the water. "Wow, you guys. That's great!"

I couldn't help wondering exactly when they'd decided all that. It felt weird to think about them having such an important conversation without me.

"Yeah." Vanessa played with her napkin, twisting it into a swanlike shape. Even when she's nervous, she's still artsy. "We figured why not give it a try?"

Kaz nodded. "Actually, we thought about beginning our romantic adventures with the marathon, but that doesn't really seem like a dating thing."

Vanessa giggled. "Besides, I'm afraid of your real girlfriend, Shani," she told Kaz.

"I don't blame you." He grinned. "I'm a little afraid of her myself. She already texted me on her mom's phone to say her entire family wants to pay to dance with me tomorrow."

I laughed along with my friends at that, but I still couldn't quite shake the strange feeling of knowing they'd been making plans without me. Was that what it would be like now that they were trying out this couple thing? Somehow I hadn't really thought about that part. What would happen once Trevor went back home—would I turn into a third wheel in their new relationship?

The thought was disturbing, but I decided not to worry about it. At least now I could talk guilt-free about Trevor in front of Kaz.

"Okay," I said as a waitress flung several menus at us on her way past the booth. "Let's pick our food, and then I'll tell you all about Trevor."

I leaned forward, peering out the car window as my dad pulled to the curb in front of the movie theater. The place was always busy on Saturday evenings, and there were tons of people milling around.

"Is your friend here?" Dad asked, idling the engine.

"I don't see him yet," I lied. Actually, I'd spotted Trevor right away. He was leaning against the wall nearby, his hands shoved into the pockets of his jeans. Looking impossibly cute, of course. "I'm sure he'll be here soon."

The last thing I wanted was for Dad to decide he wanted to get out and say hi. He tends to act like he's the world's funniest stand-up comedian when he talks to my friends, which is cute when his victims are Vanessa and Kaz. But I didn't want to spend half our date explaining his goofiness to Trevor.

Speaking of Vanessa and Kaz, I was still kind of freaked out by their big announcement. Sure, it had been all my idea for them to get together. Now that it was happening, though, I was going to have to adjust.

Fortunately, I had Trevor to distract me in the meantime. I couldn't wait to see him again.

"Okay. Call me if you need a ride home later," Dad said.

"Will do." I opened the car door and grabbed my purse. "But I'm sure Trevor's cousin is going to drop me off. They have to go practically right past our house on their way back. Thanks for the ride here, though."

"Welcome. Have fun."

With a little wave, I shut the car door and waited until he drove off. Then I turned and hurried toward Trevor, who was staring at a movie poster and hadn't seen me yet.

I called his name when I got closer, and he turned and smiled at me. Whoa, swoon—I went a little weak in the knees. But somehow I managed to stay on my feet and make it over to him.

"Hi," he said. "I was starting to worry you wouldn't get here in time. I got us tickets to the show that starts in, like, five minutes."

"Oh cool." I was touched he was being such a gentleman about buying my ticket, though I was a little surprised he hadn't asked which movie I wanted to see. What if he'd chosen something I'd already seen?

Luckily, though, he hadn't. In fact, I'd barely heard of the movie he'd chosen. It was a subtitled foreign film—not exactly my usual type of thing.

Not that I was opposed to a little culture. Especially when it came with a side dish of Trevor.

"Great, thanks." I took the ticket he handed me, shivering as our fingers touched briefly. "Should we go in?"

Okay, so maybe culture is overrated. The movie started out kind of dull and went downhill from there. At least excitement-wise.

But I didn't really mind. Because about half an hour in, Trevor started shifting in his seat beside me. For a second I thought he was about to get up to go to the bathroom or buy more popcorn or something. But then I felt his hand touch mine—and wrap itself around my fingers.

I practically hyperventilated when I realized what was happening. Holding hands, I thought, little pinwheels of happiness bursting in my brain. *We're totally holding hands! I wish Vanessa could see this. . . .*

But I didn't waste much time thinking about my friend. Instead I focused on the feel of Trevor's hand in mine. It was warm, his skin soft except for some funny little callouses on the ends of his fingers I quickly realized must come from playing guitar. I rubbed one of the callouses with my own finger, and he turned and smiled at me in the darkness.

I smiled back and held my breath, knowing what usually came next in these situations. Oh, not from firsthand experience or anything—like I've mentioned, this whole boyfriend-dating thing was all new to me. But I'd seen enough movies and TV shows to wonder—was he going to kiss me?

I leaned in a little closer, hoping my breath was okay, and closed my eyes. Then I waited . . . and waited. I squeezed his hand to let him know I was ready. He squeezed back, but still nothing happened.

Finally I cracked one eye open. Trevor was still holding my hand, but he'd turned away again to stare at the screen.

Oops. Kind of a bummer, but I tried not to worry about it. Maybe this was just Trevor being a gentleman again. Maybe holding hands was enough—at least for now.

"Want another bite?" Trevor speared half a ravioli and held it out to me.

"Thanks." I smiled and then leaned forward so he could pop it into my mouth.

The movie had ended almost an hour ago, and dinner was going well. Really well. We hadn't stopped talking since we'd left the theater, pretty much. It was great! We'd discussed the movie, reminisced some more about camp, chatted about our current favorite songs and stuff, and now we were talking about Trevor's band.

I dabbed my mouth with my napkin and then took a sip of my iced tea. "So what were you saying about the bass player?" I asked.

He laughed. "Oh right. I was just saying it's so obvious the poor guy has a massive crush on Zoe."

Right. Come to think of it, he'd been talking about Zoe kind of a lot so far. Maybe that was natural, since she was new. But I'll admit it: It was starting to bug me a little.

"So the bass player," I said, trying to sound casual. "Think he'll hook up with her?"

"Hope not." Shaking his head, he picked up his water glass. "I mean, she's hot and all, but we don't need some kind of Yoko situation messing things up just when we're really getting somewhere, you know?"

"Yoko?" I said blankly, trying not to focus on the word *hot*.

"Yoko Ono?" He shrugged. "Most people think she's the one who broke up the Beatles."

"Oh." The Beatles were more Kaz's territory than mine. I was about to say so when I heard someone calling my name.

"Chloe! Hey!" it came again.

I looked up in surprise. Maya was hurrying toward our table, Tank lumbering along behind her.

"Hi, guys," I said, taking in Maya's cute skirt and heels and Tank's tie, which barely seemed to make it around his massive neck. "Date night, huh?"

"Yeah. You too?" Maya was gazing curiously at Trevor.

"Wait." Tank scratched his broad chin, looking confused. "I thought you were going out with Kaz now, Chloe?"

I froze, shooting Maya a panicky glance. She poked Tank in his beefy bicep. "No, I told you, they're not going to the dance together after all." She shot Trevor her charming cheerleader smile. "You must be the future rock star we've heard so much about."

"Oh, right, sorry." I was feeling flustered, but I did my best to recover. "Trevor O'Brien, this is Maya Aratani, and that's Tank Riggs."

"Yo." Tank still looked a little confused. "What's up, man?"

"Not much." Trevor stood and shook Tank's hand. The effect was like watching a mouse shake hands with an elephant, which should have amused me. But I was too worried about what Trevor might be thinking. It was hard to tell, since his smile looked as cool and relaxed as always.

"Well, we should let you two get back to your date," Maya said. "Come on, Tank. The hostess is waiting for us." They both said good-bye and wandered off to their own table.

I glanced at Trevor. "About that," I said. "Um, you're probably wondering what they were talking about with the whole dance thing, right? Sorry, I should have told you about what happened. I mean, if we're going to have a—a thing together, we shouldn't have any secrets, right? The thing is, Kaz asked me to the dance."

"Kaz?" Trevor echoed with a slight frown.

"Yeah. But it was before we knew you were coming, and I probably wasn't going to say yes anyway," I hurried on.

"Probably?" The frown was a little deeper. "Look, Chloe. If there's someone you like around here, I don't have to—"

"No!" I blurted out, desperate to make him understand. To not ruin this super-romantic first date. "We're just friends. Kaz and I, that is. I mean, I've known the guy since we were in diapers—he's like a brother to me!"

"Wait." Trevor's expression cleared. "Kaz? Is that the guy you've told me about—the geeky band dork you're always hanging around with?"

Now it was my turn to frown. "I wouldn't describe him that way," I said. "But that's him, yeah."

"Sorry—no offense." Trevor held up both hands, palms out, and grinned sheepishly. "It's just that for a second there, I thought we were talking about, you know, another guy. Not just a friend."

I narrowed my eyes, not sure I liked the way he'd said the word *friend*. With an odd little grin, as if there were something wrong with Kaz, somehow.

"Um . . . ," I began.

I guess he could tell I was getting annoyed, because he leaned across the table and took my hand. "I'm sorry, Chloe," he said softly, gazing at me, his green eyes glowing with sincerity. "I'm an idiot. It's just that I was picturing a different kind of guy when that big dude was talking, you know?" With one last squeeze, he dropped my hand and sat back, picking up his fork. "One more like, well, me, I guess. I mean, Kaz just doesn't sound like the type of guy I'd hang out with or whatever, so I wasn't picturing him with—Well, anyway, sorry. Are we cool?"

I took a deep breath, telling myself not to be stupid and overreact. Trevor had no idea how defensive I was of my friends. We were just getting to know each other again, still feeling each other out, which meant there were bound to be misunderstandings.

Besides, I was sure Kaz would think I was crazy to freak out over Trevor's comments. What had he said, anyway? That Kaz was a geek? Kaz himself wore the label proudly.

"Sure, we're cool." I sipped my water, eyeing Trevor over the rim of the glass. As I set it down, I smiled. "Anyway, you'll change your mind about Kaz once you get to know him. Everyone loves him. I mean, you're both music lovers, right?"

"Sure." Trevor speared another ravioli.

That reminded me. . . . "Maybe you can hang out with him some at the marathon tomorrow," I continued. "Did you find out yet if you can come?"

"It's tomorrow?"

"Uh-huh. Starts at noon, but I'll there helping with the final setup stuff from around ten thirty or so." I maintained my pleasant smile, trying not to look impatient with his question, even though I'd already told him the answer half a dozen times.

He shrugged. "That should work," he said. "Text me the directions, and I'll see if Jon'll drop me off."

"Really?" I was so thrilled that I almost knocked over my iced tea. "Awesome! We'll have a blast, I promise."

"Cool." He smiled at me over his water glass. "So anyway, what were we talking about before your friends stopped by?"

"The band," I said with a smile. "And how you guys are just about to hit it big if there's no Yoko action . . ."

The rest of the dinner was amazing. We clicked so well, it felt like our tenth date instead of our first. Well, except it was super-romantic, like first dates are supposed to be. I could have sat there forever over our cooling plates of pasta. Unfortunately, Jon texted before we could even think about ordering dessert, telling Trevor he'd be there to get us soon.

Oh well. At least I could look forward to hanging out with Trevor all day at the marathon. He paid for dinner, which was sweet, and then we headed outside.

Jon pulled up less than five minutes later. I was sort of hoping Trevor and I would both sit in the backseat so we could hold hands again on the way back into town. Unfortunately, that thought didn't seem to occur to Trevor, since he headed for the front passenger side. With a shrug, I reached for the door behind him.

"Wait," Jon said, twisting around and frowning at me when I slid into the backseat. "Am I supposed to drive you somewhere too?"

"Oh, sorry." Trevor shot me an apologetic look. "Um, can you drop off Chloe at her house when we go back through town?"

"It's right on the way." I shot Jon my most winning smile as I told him my address.

Jon didn't look thrilled, but he shrugged. "Whatever."

We didn't talk much on the short drive to town, mostly because Jon was blaring some terrible rap station on the radio. When he stopped in front of my house, I reached for the door.

"Thanks for the ride," I said, raising my voice to be heard above the music.

"Wait." Trevor opened his door and jumped back to help me finish opening mine. Then he held out his hand with a smile. "Walk you to the door?"

"Hurry up, Prince Charming!" Jon shouted from the driver's seat. "I don't have all night."

Trevor ignored him, squeezing my hand. I squeezed back, smiling up at him. "Thanks," I said.

We headed up the front walk, hand in hand. It felt perfect—like a line from the song. When we reached the porch, we paused in front of the door and kind of looked at each other. The porch light was full of dead bugs, which I normally thought was totally gross. But tonight I was glad of it, since it made the light dim and weirdly romantic, at least if I didn't think too much about it.

"Well, thanks for everything," I said softly. "This was fun."

"Yeah." He smiled down at me.

I held my breath. Okay, maybe he hadn't kissed me in the movie theater. But this time I was *sure* I knew what happened next. And I was pretty sure he knew it too. I hoped my breath wasn't too garlicky after all that pasta. Then again he'd had garlic too, so no worries. . . .

The soundtrack was already playing in my head as we stood there, still smiling at each other.

You'll share a first kiss if you dare.
Remember it always: True romance is rare.

He leaned a little closer. "So I guess this is where we . . . ," he began in a husky, sexy voice.

Gobble, gobble, gobble!

The sound of an excited turkey rang out in the still night air, startling both of us. Trevor dropped my hand and jumped back.

"What was that?" he blurted out, staring around as if expecting a flock of gobblers to leap out of the darkness.

I grimaced, grabbing my phone out of my bag. "Sorry," I said, quickly silencing it. "Just a funny text tone."

I didn't bother to tell him it was one Kaz found so hilarious that he was always programming it in for himself in my phone, even though I kept changing it back to something a little less obnoxious. Usually I thought it was funny when he did that. Right now? Not so much. Talk about a mood killer!

Trevor was already moving toward the porch steps, his hands in his pockets. "This was fun," he called over his shoulder. "See you tomorrow."

"Yeah." My heart sank as I realized our first kiss would have to wait. But so what? We had all week to make it happen. "Don't forget to get there early if you want to help us set up. And be sure to bring your guitar!"

He lifted a hand without turning around, disappearing back into Jon's car a moment later. I stood in the dim, bug-shadowed light and watched until the car's taillights disappeared into the night.

Chapter Twelve

When I walked into the gym the next morning, Maya was already there barking orders like a drill sergeant. She spotted me right away.

"Chloe," she said, hurrying over. "Kaz the spaz dropped the sheet music all over the place just now when he was supposed to be taking it to make copies. Can you go help him get organized?"

"On it," I agreed.

I looked around, pausing for just a moment to admire the work we'd done the day before. The gym looked amazing. Kaz's idea had been to decorate it in the style of a shabby old hotel ballroom, like the one in the old movie he'd seen about a dance marathon during the Great Depression. But the Depression wasn't exactly the most cheerful thing in the world, so some of the other organizers had favored more of a sock hop vibe, since Kaz had also told us there was a dance marathon on an episode of *Happy Days*. We'd ended up with sort of a fusion—Kaz had donated his disco ball to the cause and begged several local antique shops to loan us some stuffy old upholstered chairs and stuff. One of the cheerleaders had liberated a bunch of vinyl albums from her dad's stash, which were taped to the walls, along with homemade posters that said DANCE! in bright colors. There were streamers and balloons, and someone had even brought in a couple of big fake potted palm trees that stood on either side of the sign-in table. Basically the place looked wacky and a little confusing—but fun.

At least a dozen of the other volunteers were already there, and they looked wacky but fun, too. Kaz had told us that dance marathons were popular from the 1920s through the 1960s or so, and most people had dressed up in costumes from one of those eras. Vanessa had reused her flapper dress from last Halloween, several of the guys were wearing Al Capone–style gangster costumes or zoot suits, and Maya looked adorable in a puffy pink poodle skirt.

As for me? I'd opted for a combination of costume and cute. My flapper dress had a big rip in it from an impromptu game of tag and a spiky shrub in Vanessa's front yard, and I wasn't sure Trevor would be impressed with the look anyway. So I'd borrowed a full black skirt from my mom, pairing it with a sparkly silver top and my favorite ballet flats.

Speaking of Trevor, I hadn't heard from him yet that morning. I pulled out my phone and sent him a quick text to let him know I was at the marathon. Then I continued on my way.

Vanessa was over by the refreshment table, helping some of the others arrange cookies and brownies on trays. I gave her a quick wave as I passed, and then I headed to the bandstand. That was what we were calling the circle of chairs we'd set up for the musicians under one of the basketball hoops.

When I arrived, Kaz was bent over a huge mess of sheet music lying on the floor, digging through it with Cody, a senior saxophone player. My favorite sax player, actually, since he was the one who'd convinced Mr. Graves to let us perform a hip-hop medley at the spring concert last year, which had been absolutely hilarious. Normally Cody was pretty laid back, but at the moment his dark brown eyes were anxious. Kaz just looked disgruntled.

"Hi," I said. "Maya sent me over to help."

Kaz glanced up. He was wearing a snazzy vintage suit I hadn't seen before, his black hair slicked back. "Great," he said. "Grab the playlist and read it out to us so we can put the music back in the right order."

I picked up the stapled sheaf of papers he'd indicated. We'd all come up with the playlist at one of the earlier meetings, creating a fun list of songs we thought would entertain people who came to watch or participate in the dancing.

"We already found the first four pieces," Cody said. "We're looking for 'Sing, Sing, Sing' right now."

"Okay. Watch for the disco medley while you're at it," I said. "That's next."

Cody shuffled through the loose pages on the floor. "We have to hurry," he said. "We still need to make copies of everything for the whole band."

"We can do it," Kaz said. "If we're still working on it when this thing starts, the band can always play 'The Stars and Stripes Forever.' We all know that one by heart, right?"

I laughed. That particular Sousa march had to be Mr. Graves's favorite song ever. The marching band had played it every single year for as long as anyone could remember.

"Let's hope we don't have to resort to that," I joked. "It's not much of a dance tune." I scanned down the list as I waited for them to find the music they were looking for. "Speaking of which, are we sure we really want to play the Rossini? That could be hard to dance to too."

"You mean the 'William Tell Overture'?" Cody shrugged. "That was actually the cheerleaders' idea—they thought it could be fun for the kids."

Kaz laughed. "Yeah. I think the term Maya used was *up-tempo*."

"Hmm." I could just imagine what Trevor would say when he got a load of our playlist, with its weird mix of modern songs, show tunes, kiddie pop, and classic concert band arrangements. "With the whole 1950s thing going on, maybe we should add, like, the theme from *Happy Days*, or maybe some old rock songs or whatever. I'm sure I could find sheet music on the Internet."

Kaz looked surprised. "*You* want to add some vintage rock?" he said. "No argument here. We could use it to replace 'True Cliché.'"

"We are *not* ditching 'True Romance,'" I informed him, sticking out my tongue. I'd lobbied hard to get that song included, and I wasn't about to back down on it now—especially with Trevor coming. "But I think a little more of a rock 'n' roll vibe could be fun, right? Maybe Trevor could even do a guitar solo."

I threw the last part in casually, not sure how Kaz would react. He didn't—at least, not really. His eyes stayed on the mess of paper as he let out sort of a humph.

"Who's Trevor?" Cody asked.

"My, um . . ." I shot a look at Kaz. "A friend of mine who's visiting from out of town. He's a really amazing guitarist, so I asked Maya if he could sit in with us."

That was true. I'd texted her the night before after my date. She'd texted back right away, saying it was fine.

"Whatever," Kaz said. "Let's worry about it after we get this music in order. Hey, here's the disco medley."

"Give it here. I'll add it to the stack." I held out my hand. Kaz jumped to his feet and handed it to me. At least that was probably what he meant to do. What he actually did was lunge to a semi-standing position, immediately slip on some loose sheets of music, and come flying straight toward me.

"Look out!" Cody cried, diving out of the way.

My reflexes weren't as fast as his. "Oof!" I grunted as Kaz hit me square in the midsection, sending us both flying.

The pile of music broke my fall, at least a little. Kaz landed right on top of me, knocking all the air out of my lungs.

"Ouch!" I yelped as his elbow banged me in the hip.

"Sorry!" he cried at the same time, trying to roll aside.

"Wait!" Cody said. "Stop. Your cuff link is caught in her skirt. If you yank your arm away . . ." He shrugged, not bothering to go into detail.

"Hold still," I ordered Kaz, trying to remember which underpants I'd put on that day. Reaching down carefully past his torso, I scrabbled for the cuff link.

"Don't break it," Kaz said. "I borrowed it from my uncle."

I rolled my eyes at him. At least I started to—his face was so close to mine, it was a little unnerving.

Not that it should have been. I mean, it was Kaz, and we were totally over that whole awkward let's-go-out phase, right? I was with Trevor, he was with Vanessa, all was right with the world. . . .

Still, I was way too aware of his heart beating against mine, and the scent of his shampoo filling my nostrils. I felt my face starting to go red and I muttered at him for a second time to hold still as I reached again for the cuff link.

At that moment a couple of guys from the brass section wandered past. "Get a room, you two!" one of them yelled.

The other let out a wolf whistle. "Way to go, Kaz-man!" he exclaimed.

"Shut up!" I told them through gritted teeth. Kaz didn't say anything, but when I glanced at him out of the corner of my eye, his face was looking decidedly lobsterlike.

The two brass players laughed and moved on.

"Need help?" Cody asked, leaning closer.

"I've got it." Luckily, my fingers are pretty nimble from years of playing the clarinet, and I soon had the cuff link loose. "There," I said, hoping my—er, Mom's—skirt didn't have a hole in it now. "Got it."

"Thanks." Kaz stayed where he was for a second, looking down at me. "Sorry about that, Chloe."

"It's okay. But you can get off me now, all right?" I gave him a little shove.

Soon we were on our feet again. I smoothed down my skirt, and Kaz fiddled with his cuff link while Cody surveyed the mess we'd made. "If you two wanted to cuddle, you could've chosen a more convenient place," he said.

"If that's what you consider cuddling, you have a problem," I informed him, trying not to let myself start blushing even harder. Seriously, when were people going to get that Kaz and I were just friends? Maybe seeing him and Vanessa at the school dance together would help.

"Come on." Kaz didn't bother to respond to Cody's comment. He was already crouching down by the messed-up pile. "Let's get back to it before Maya strangles us all."

That seemed like a good plan. Working together, the three of us finally got the music sorted and organized. Then Cody rushed off to the school office to make copies, while Kaz and I headed over to ask Maya what else needed to be done.

"Sorry again about, you know, tackling you before," he said

with a sidelong glance at me. "Guess it's a good thing your boyfriend isn't here yet, or he might get the wrong idea. You know, like those guys obviously did."

"Those guys are idiots," I muttered. "You could've killed me."

"So, speaking of the amazing Trevor, is he really showing up today?" Kaz's voice was light and casual. "Guess I'll have to eat my words about him not being real."

"Yep. He should be here anytime now." I pulled out my phone, but he hadn't returned my text yet. Checking my watch, I realized it was almost eleven thirty. "Actually, I should make sure he didn't sneak in and get put to work by your crazy cousin when I wasn't looking."

As Kaz continued toward Maya, I rushed off in search of Trevor. But two rounds of the gym later, he was nowhere to be found. Vanessa came up behind me while I was peeking out into the hallway.

"What are you doing?" she asked, tucking a loose strand of blond hair back under her flapper hat.

"Looking for Trevor." I took out my phone again. Still no response. I texted him again.

Getting close to go time! U getting here soon? Can't wait to see u!

"I'm sure he'll be here soon," Vanessa said. "In the meantime, I'm supposed to open up another box of napkins and put them out. Want to help?"

"Sure." Casting one more glance up and down the deserted hallway, I followed her back inside.

The next half hour passed quickly. There were a million little last-minute things to do, from testing the lemonade dispenser to sweeping the dance floor to setting out the copied sheet music on the stands. Maya was like a whirling dervish as she raced around, supervising everything.

But by the time the bus had arrived with the S&D kids, we were ready. Well, almost. Trevor still hadn't arrived.

"Yo, Chloe!" Carlos was bright-eyed and snazzy looking as he danced over to me in his pinstripe suit and fedora. "You gonna dance with me today?"

"Only if you cough up some dough, buddy," I told him with a grin.

"No way," he retorted. "People pay to dance with *me*, not the other way around!" He did a spin and tipped his hat.

I laughed. "How can I resist your moves?" I said. "I'd pay anything to dance with you, C-man! I'll have to see if I can sneak away from the band long enough to boogie with you."

"That's more like it." He grinned and then rushed off to say hi to some of the others.

A few minutes later more people started to arrive. Before long at least a couple dozen of them had already signed up for dances, and lots of others—parents, friends, siblings—were mobbing the refreshments table or hanging out on the sidelines, talking to the kids or watching the musicians put together their instruments. Which reminded me—I needed to get warmed up myself. But first I had to figure out what had happened to Trevor.

As I pulled out my phone again to check for new texts, Maya grabbed a microphone, her voice ringing out over the gym as she ordered the band to take their seats and the cheerleaders to hit the dance floor. Cheers and whistles rang out from all corners as everyone obeyed. A girl from the orchestra sat down at the harp and strummed a few strings, and one of the percussionists crashed his cymbals together, making several people jump. The familiar random sounds of a band warming up rang out through the gym.

There were no texts from Trevor. I swung past the door to check the hallway, then sat down and quickly fitted my clarinet together.

"Where's Mr. Wonderful?" Kaz asked, pausing by my chair on his way back to join the other brass players.

I tootled a few warm-up notes on my clarinet before answering. "I'm sure he'll be here," I said. "He has to get his cousin to drive him, so maybe they got delayed."

"That's probably it," Vanessa said from her seat across the way with the other flutes. "I bet he'll be here any second."

"Hmm." Kaz pursed his lips. "I was only kidding before about thinking this Trevor guy doesn't actually exist. Now I'm not so sure."

"Go sit down already." I frowned at him. "We're getting ready to start."

As he grinned and loped off, I checked my phone again. Nothing.

"Text me something, would you?" I called to Vanessa.

She looked up from her instrument. "Huh?"

"Text me something—doesn't matter what. I want to see if my phone's working."

She blinked, then nodded and dug her phone out of the bag under her chair. Seconds later my phone vibrated, and I saw her text pop up.

Testing blah blah ☺

"Did it work?" she called.

I just nodded, chewing my lower lip as I tried to decide whether to text Trevor again. Where could he be? I hoped nothing bad had happened. What if he'd been in an accident on his way here or something? Come to think of it, Jon hadn't struck me as the best driver in the world. . . .

The phone vibrated in my hand, startling me so my clarinet almost rolled off my lap. It was Trevor!

"About time," I muttered, touching the screen to bring up the text.

Hey, C, looks like I won't be able to make your fundraising thing after all. Sorry, family stuff, blah! Lol. Have fun tho, okay?

I stared at the words, disappointment washing over me. Followed by annoyance.

"You couldn't have told me this sooner?" I muttered.

One of the percussionists stepped to the front of the band. We were all supposed to take turns conducting, and he'd drawn the first turn.

"Everyone ready?" he said.

"Hold up a sec." I jumped out of my seat and stepped toward the conductor. "Listen, uh, I'd stuck in notes on a couple of the songs about my friend doing a guitar solo, but it turns out he can't make it. So, um, ignore them, okay?"

The conductor looked a little confused, but he nodded. "Okay, whatever. Go sit down, Chloe—we're already late getting started."

I dashed back to my seat and raised my clarinet to my lips. Across the way, I saw Vanessa shooting me a curious look. I lowered my instrument and mouthed the words *He's not coming*, though I wasn't sure she got it. Meanwhile, out in the middle of the gym, Maya still had the microphone.

"Without further ado," she said loudly, "let the dance marathon begin!"

The kids all let out a cheer, and several of the other cheerleaders whooped and did little cheerleadery leaps and kicks. The conductor raised his hands and we started to play, our first few notes all but drowned out by applause and shouts from the crowd. I watched the dance floor out of the corner of my eye. Within seconds every cheerleader seemed to be out there twirling around with someone. All the kids were dancing too. Most of them had paying customers, though a few were dancing with one another. I smiled as I spotted Aidan smiling shyly up at his partner, who happened to be Vanessa's mom. I was glad to see him—I'd been so distracted looking for Trevor that I hadn't had a chance to greet most of the S&D kids.

But now I looked around as I played, loving how much fun everyone was having. The other dance floor was crowded with people of all ages shaking and shimmying and laughing as they moved to the rhythm we were laying down. It looked like fun, and for a second I wished I could be out there with them.

But as much as I loved dancing, I loved playing music even more. My fingers flew over the keys of my clarinet as we finished the first song and launched into the second.

For the next half hour or so I forgot everything except wringing every last note I could out of my instrument. Each time I glanced out toward the dance floor, it looked more crowded with people dancing and laughing and having a blast. About forty minutes in we finally paused for a break.

"Take five, everyone!" the conductor called out. "Next conductor's up when we get back."

"That's me!" Cody called out.

I set down my clarinet and hurried over to the small table by the bandstand where we'd set up water bottles and lemonade. Grabbing some water, I downed half the bottle in one gulp.

Kaz and Vanessa joined me. "This is fun, isn't it?" Kaz exclaimed.

Vanessa laughed and plucked at his hair, which had escaped from its gel and was sticking up at odd angles. "Definitely," she said.

He smiled down at her, and I averted my eyes, suddenly feeling awkward. They really were an adorable couple. . . .

Kaz glanced at me. "So, where is he?"

I didn't need to ask who he meant. I took another gulp of water before answering. "He can't make it after all. Family stuff or whatever."

"Really? Sorry, Chloe." Vanessa squeezed my arm, looking sympathetic.

Kaz shrugged. "Yeah, bummer, Chloe," he said. "I know you were all excited." He actually sounded sincere, which I appreciated. I wasn't sure I could take any more teasing about my imaginary almost-boyfriend right then.

"Yeah. Well, whatever, thanks. Let's not talk about it anymore, okay?" I shot a look around. "Can you believe how many people are here?"

It seemed as if everyone in town had turned out for the marathon. I spotted several of my neighbors, my bus driver, and one of the hair stylists from the salon my mom and I went to, along with Vanessa's parents and little sister, who was giggling as one of the cheerleaders twirled her around. My own family had promised to stop by after Timothy's soccer scrimmage.

"Look, I see my dentist over there!" Vanessa exclaimed. She grinned widely. "Do my teeth look okay?"

I laughed. "Chill. I doubt he's planning to give you an exam right here and now."

Maya rushed over just then, flinging her arms around Kaz and hugging him so hard, his eyes practically bugged out. "Dude, you're a genius!" she exclaimed. "We're already more than halfway to our money goal, and it's only, like, one o'clock! Can you believe it?"

"Definitely," I said. "We already knew Kaz was a genius."

Kaz laughed breathlessly. "Did we? Someone should tell Ms. Farley. She gave me a C plus on my last test."

Maya ignored that, letting go of her cousin and racing off to hug one of the other cheerleaders who was sucking down lemonade nearby.

"She seems happy," Vanessa said with a giggle.

I smiled, deciding not to fret over no-show Trevor anymore. Why let his stupid family and their last-minute change of plans ruin my fun? Besides, he was here all week—I was sure we'd have plenty of time together. Not to mention the school dance next Saturday. Maybe it was better if today was about the kids and my friends and having fun. After all, not everything had to be about true romance.

"Come on. Let's get back to our seats," I told my friends. "I'm ready to keep this party going!"

Two hours later the dance marathon was still in full swing. Some of the early guests had left by then, though plenty of other people had turned up to replace them. My family had come and gone, but only after I'd guilted my dad into writing a huge donation check so he didn't have to actually dance. My mom had danced once with Carlos and once with Aidan, and Timothy had taken a turn with Toni the cheerleader.

It was nice to see our hard work paying off. So nice that I didn't think about Trevor at all. Well, hardly at all, anyway. Seriously. I was way too busy having a great time.

When the conductor called for another break, Vanessa bolted from her seat. "Be right back," she called over her shoulder. "I think I drank too much water on the last break."

As she disappeared in the direction of the restrooms, I wandered over to join Kaz at the drinks table. "Running out of breath yet?" I asked, and gave him a poke in the arm. "We've got some pretty brass-heavy numbers coming up, so I hope you can handle it."

"Don't worry. I can handle anything." He grinned and struck a bodybuilder pose. Then he grabbed a bottle of water. "I just hope those poor cheerleaders' legs don't fall off from trying to keep up with all those hyper little kids."

"Hey, if they do, we can take over," I said. "We'll just have to play and dance at the same time!"

Kaz laughed. "Sounds like fun. Maybe we should suggest that for next year's fund-raiser."

"Maybe we should." I chugged some lemonade, watching Kaz out of the corner of my eye. Today was a huge success, and it never would have happened without him. He was such an amazing guy. "We could start planning it at Aesop's after the marathon—just the three of us." Suddenly realizing what I'd said, I coughed. "I mean, if you and Vanessa don't already have plans, that is. You know—just the two of you. I mean, I wouldn't want to—"

"No, it's fine," he cut me off. "I mean, we hadn't really talked about it, so . . ."

Whatever he said after that, I didn't hear it. Because I glanced in the direction of the door just in time to see Trevor walk in—carrying his guitar case and looking impossibly hot.

Chapter Thirteen

I was stunned, but I recovered quickly. "Trevor!" I yelled, waving my hands over my head. "Over here!"

Pushing through the crowd, I reached him before he'd made it more than a few steps into the gym. He flipped his hair back and smiled when he saw me.

"Chloe," he said. "Hey. Surprise! I made it after all."

"Awesome! But what happened?" I asked, hardly daring to believe he was really here. "I thought you were coming, and then I got your text. . . ."

"Yeah, sorry about that." He reached up and tucked a strand of hair behind my ear. I was so distracted by the feeling of his calloused fingers on my cheek, I got a little lost and missed what he said next.

"Uh, um, what?" I burbled, realizing he was looking at me as if expecting a response.

"I said the band called to say hi," he said. "Zoe had some ideas about our playlist they wanted to run by me, and I kind of lost track of time, and then my aunt was talking about maybe getting some food. . . ." He shrugged. "It doesn't matter. I decided I couldn't let you down, so I talked Jon into bringing me."

"I'm glad." I smiled up at him, imagining what everyone would say when they heard him play. But wait—I didn't have to imagine it. Grabbing his hand, I pulled him after me. "Come on. You're just in time—we're about to start our next set."

"Cool." He let me drag him over to the bandstand. Vanessa had returned by now, and she and Kaz were standing by her seat.

"Guys!" I exclaimed. "Check it out—come meet Trevor!"

Vanessa's jaw dropped, but Kaz hardly twitched. "So this is the famous Trevor, huh?" he said, stepping over and holding out his hand. "Kazuo Aratani, at your service."

Trevor blinked at him, then reached out his hand to shake Kaz's. "Um, hi. Chloe's told me all about you."

"*All* about me? Oh dear," Kaz said. "Then it seems I'll have to ask you to sign a confidentiality agreement."

"Ignore him. He's just being silly," I told Trevor, seeing the confusion in his eyes. Most people didn't know what to make of Kaz at first. I grabbed Vanessa and pulled her closer. She was staring at Trevor as if he were some fascinating but slightly terrifying alien species. "This is Van. Vanessa Bennett, I mean. My other best friend."

"Hi, Vanessa." Trevor smiled at her and flipped his hair back again. "Chloe's told me about you, too. It's really great to meet you."

"Hi." Vanessa was doing that shy thing again, peeking out at him from behind a curtain of blond hair. It made her look extra adorable, and I sort of wanted to hug her.

Okay, I sort of wanted to hug the world just then. Starting with a certain future rock god and almost-boyfriend whose arrival was the cherry on top of this amazing sundae of a day. Sundae—Sunday—get it?

Yeah, I was feeling a little giddy. So sue me!

Kaz was looking curiously at Trevor's guitar case. "So, dude," he said. "Chloe tells us you're a pretty good axeman. Who do you like best, Townshend, Van Halen, or Page?"

Trevor didn't miss a beat. "Hendrix," he replied. "Those other guys are cool too, though."

Kaz nodded, looking impressed. "Nice." He shot me a look. "I don't know what you were talking about, Chloe. This guy is for real. Not imaginary at all."

Once again Trevor looked a little confused. But I smiled at Kaz. "Told ya so," I said. "And thanks."

Then I grabbed Trevor by the hand, leading him over to introduce him to Maya and the current conductor, a junior French horn player named Sophie, who were huddled over the sheet music nearby. I quickly explained who he was and what he could do. Trevor helped by flashing them his cutest smile, then playing a few riffs on his guitar.

"This is good," Maya announced. "Annamaria is getting blisters from the harp, and I don't dare let Kaz take over since every time he gets near that thing, he starts playing the theme from *Deliverance*. Anyway, we could stand to mix things up a little in the stringed-instrument department. So find a place to sit, Trevor, and welcome to the chaos."

He chuckled. "Thanks."

"I think there's a free seat over there by the other guitar people." Sophie waved at a chair off to one side, where various band members had been taking turn strumming the guitars and banjos and other instruments people had brought.

Trevor thanked her and immediately headed that way. I was a little disappointed he hadn't even said anything to me before going—at least until I saw him nod at the other guitarists, grab the free chair, and start back toward me, dragging it behind him.

"Hey, mind scooting over?" he asked the clarinetist next to me, wearing a charming smile.

Said clarinetist was a quiet freshman whose name I was pretty sure was Rachel, though it was hard to be certain since she barely spoke. Decent musician, though. At Trevor's request she looked up from the book she'd been reading while waiting to get started again.

"Um . . ." she said. "Okay?"

"Cool." Trevor waited until she'd scooted over a bit, and

then he wedged his chair in between hers and mine. It was kind of a tight squeeze, and when he sat down, our thighs touched. Romantic!

He looked up at Sophie, who'd just taken her place in front of the band. "Ready when you are, boss," he called to her.

She nodded and raised her hands. "In one . . . two . . . three . . ."

I was so distracted by having Trevor right there next to me that I forgot to play for a second. But I caught myself quickly, blowing out my part for all I was worth. How long had it been since Trevor and I had made music together?

Five years, I thought. Actually, five years, eight months, and six days. But who's counting?

Okay, I was getting distracted again. I realized I'd lost my place in the song. But who cared? Music didn't have to be perfect to work. I kept the clarinet to my lips but stopped playing for a moment, instead listening to Trevor strumming softly along with the rest of the band. There was no guitar part on the music in front of us, but that didn't stop him from improvising his part. *Just like a real pro*, I thought proudly.

The next song was a recent pop-rock hit. Trevor smiled when I flipped to the music.

"This is more like it," he murmured, winking at me.

"Yeah. Hold that thought." I hopped up and stepped over to Sophie. "Hey, maybe Trev can do a guitar solo on this one?" I said softly. "Could be cool, right?"

She shrugged. "Sure, why not? Tell him to go for it."

"Thanks." I returned to my seat, grinning. "Okay, Mr. Hendrix," I said quietly. "You up for a rocking solo?"

He raised an eyebrow. "Always."

Sophie started the song then, so we had to stop talking. When we reached the part where the guitarist took over in the recorded version of the song, Trevor jumped to his feet and stepped to the front of the band as he wailed up and down the frets. A few people whooped and stomped their feet or clapped. One of the percussionists tapped his sticks together to keep the beat. But mostly all eyes and ears were on Trevor as he did his thing.

I wasn't sure whether to close my eyes to better soak up the sound, or keep them open to enjoy the view. I settled for some of each. It was amazing! The solo went on . . . and on . . . and then on some more. Once or twice I saw some of the other musicians raise their instruments as if thinking it was time to jump in again. But I could read Trevor's body language as easily as an ABC book, and I could tell he was so into it that he wasn't planning on stopping anytime soon. Which was fine with me. I could have watched him play all night.

But finally Sophie raised her hands. "Okay, guys!" she said over the sound of the wailing guitar. The band started playing the chorus again, and Trevor finished up and sat down.

He was breathing hard, but he looked happy. "Okay, that was fun," he told me. "How'd I sound?"

"Incredible!" I said, grabbing his hand and squeezing it. "I wish I'd thought to record it on my phone."

He grinned. "That's okay. Maybe I'll play it for you again later."

I blushed but didn't say anything, mostly because the song had just ended. Reaching for my stand, I switched to the next piece of music, a lively number from *Guys and Dolls* that had brought the house down at our last concert.

Trevor wrinkled his nose when he saw it. "I think I blew my wad on that solo just now," he said. "Come on, let's go dance for a while."

"Huh?" I was too surprised to react as he yanked me to my feet. Handing off my clarinet to Rachel on my way past, I followed him out toward the dance floor.

"Hey," Sophie called. "Where are you going?"

"Dancing." I laughed, loving Trevor's impulsiveness. How romantic was it that he couldn't control the urge to dance with *me*?

Sophie shrugged and lifted her hands to begin the song. Most of the band started playing on cue, though a few people were watching us instead.

"Hey," one of the trombone players yelled out after a few bars. "My lips are numb. I want to dance too!"

"Yeah," a percussionist called out, dropping his sticks on the snare with a clatter. "Come on, people. Let's boogie!"

"What are you doing?" Maya let go of her dance partner and hurried toward us.

"What does it look like?" I told her with a grin. "We're dancing!"

Within seconds there was a full-out riot from the band. People were setting down their instruments left and right, leaving only a handful of musicians still playing.

"How are we going to dance without music?" one of the cheerleaders complained.

Toni giggled. "Maybe we should play!" She ran over and grabbed someone's saxophone, blowing into it and producing a loud squawk. Several other cheerleaders also headed for the bandstand. One of them started strumming randomly on the harp, while another crashed the cymbals together, and a third actually blared out a few notes on a trumpet. The people who'd come to dance or watch seemed a little confused, though most of them were still dancing through it all.

"Dude!" Carlos cried. "You guys stink. I can play better than that!" He grabbed the drumsticks from a cheerleader, who, laughing, backed off and let him take over. Several other kids also took over various instruments. Despite all the music lessons we'd given them over the past year, the result was pure musical chaos.

Trevor and I stood there watching the show. He chuckled as two little girls started arguing over the banjo. "Things suddenly got much more rock 'n' roll around here," he told me with a grin. "You're welcome."

I laughed, though I felt slightly worried by the stormy expression on Maya's face as she headed for the bandstand.

Suddenly Kaz leaped into view in the middle of the dance floor. "Yo, I'm here to save the day!" he cried, holding up his phone. He punched a button, and music poured out—namely, a popular recent dance tune.

"That's more like it!" one of Vanessa's fellow flutists cried, grooving to the beat.

I relaxed against Trevor as everyone else started dancing too—including Maya. "Hey, aren't we supposed to be dancing?" I said, tilting my head up to smile at him.

He took both of my hands and spun me around. "Your wish is my command."

The rest of the marathon was pure anarchic fun. People took turns playing their favorite songs on their phones and MP3 players, and someone even found a speaker to plug them into so everyone could hear better. The band members volunteered to dance with the paying customers right along with the kids and cheerleaders so everyone could get as many turns as they wanted.

Well, *most* of the band volunteered, anyway. I wasn't about to give up the super-awesome dance partner I already had. Trevor was almost as amazing a dancer as he was a guitarist. He spun me around, shook his hips, and generally seemed to be having just as much fun as I was. The only slight bummer was nobody seemed too interested in playing any slow songs, keeping things almost frenetically up-tempo.

But I could live with that. We would be right back here in the gym next weekend at the big dance, and there were sure to be plenty of slow songs then. This taste of dancing with Trevor just made me look forward to the big night even more.

Things were starting to wind down by ten of seven. Trevor and I took a break from dancing to grab some drinks. As we stood there watching Kaz do his usual goofy spaz dance in the middle of the floor, I glanced up at Trevor, still hardly believing he was really there.

"This has been great," I said. "I'm glad you made it after all."

"Yeah, me too." He chugged some lemonade.

I was about to invite him to join my friends and me at the diner after the marathon when someone shouted his name. Glancing toward the door, I saw that it was Jon. And he didn't look happy.

Trevor heard him too. "Oops," he said, grabbing my arm to check my watch. "Lost track of the time. I'd better go."

He took off toward Jon before I could respond. I watched him go, a little disappointed . . . at least until he paused just long enough to smile and blow me a kiss.

I shivered, wishing it were the real thing as he disappeared through the door. But that would come soon enough. After all the super-romantic moments with Trevor this weekend, I was sure of that. Spotting Carlos grooving to the beat nearby, I grinned and headed over to demand the dance he'd promised me.

I was in the world's best mood an hour or so later as my friends and I helped clean up the gym. The kids had just piled back onto their bus for the long drive back to the city, and Vanessa and I were dismantling the last of the decorations behind the bandstand. "This was amazing," I said to her for about the millionth time.

"I know, right?" She shot me a sly look. "By the way, did I mention Trevor is even better looking in person?"

I giggled. "Oh, eight or nine times, yeah," I said. "But feel free to keep mentioning it as often as you want."

Maya was with Kaz and a few other people over at the sign-in table. Suddenly she clapped her hands and whistled loudly for attention.

"Okay, it's official!" she called out. "We totally smashed our goals!"

"Woo-hoo!" Cody shouted, pumping his fist. "New solid gold music stands for everyone!"

I laughed along with everyone else. Maya grinned. "Give yourselves a round of applause," she added, causing the place to erupt with cheers, whistles, and stomping feet. When the noise started to fade, she grabbed Kaz and dragged him forward, lifting his arm in the air as if he'd just won a boxing match. "And another round of applause for my genius cousin whose brainstorm started it all!"

"Yay, Kaz!" I screamed. The rest of the crowd was cheering and shouting too. Kaz waved and bowed and grinned and basically ate it all up like the huge ham he is, which only made everyone cheer even louder.

Just then the janitor appeared and started shooing us all toward the door.

"I can take care of the rest, kids," he said. "Now get out of here already."

I grabbed Vanessa's hand so we wouldn't get separated in the sudden stampede. "Come on," I told her. "Let's go find Kaz and celebrate this incredible day with some grease and sugar at Aesop's."

Chapter Fourteen

When I woke up on Monday morning, the first thing I did was grab my phone. I'd been pretty beat by the time I got home from Aesop's the previous night, but before falling into bed I'd texted Trevor to ask about getting together again soon. We'd talked about it a little on Saturday night, but I'd totally forgotten to bring it up at the marathon.

And no wonder. I still smiled every time I flashed back to the moment I'd seen him walk into the gym. And the moment he'd stood up and started that incredible solo. And when he'd pulled me out onto the dance floor and when he'd blown me that kiss and, well, pretty much every moment we'd been together.

I couldn't wait for more. My mind was full of true romance as I tapped in my password.

There were several new texts waiting for me—one from Kaz, two from Vanessa, and a group text from Maya, thanking everyone who'd participated in the fund-raiser.

But nothing from Trevor. I frowned, scrolling over to make sure I hadn't imagined sending him that text last night. No—there it was, glowing on the screen.

Today was fun! Want to hang out tomorrow like we talked about? Text me and we'll figure out the details. Chat soon! ☺

"Oh well," I muttered. "Maybe he's sleeping in."

That had to be it. If I didn't have to go to school, I definitely wouldn't be up yet either, especially after my busy Sunday. He'd probably get back to me in an hour or two. Dropping my phone into my purse, I yawned and headed across the hall for a shower.

Trevor finally texted me back right before lunchtime. I felt the phone vibrate in my pocket during geometry class, but I didn't dare check it until Ms. Feldman released us at the bell.

I darted into the hall but stopped short as soon as I read the message. Vanessa was coming out after me and almost stepped on my heel.

"Hey," she said. "What's wrong?"

I held up the phone so she could see the text: *Can't get together today, sorry. Jon cut school so we can head over to check out a vintage record place in Smithton. We're leaving in a few, but I'll text u tonight. Maybe we can do something tomorrow.*

"Smithton?" Vanessa said.

I nodded. That was a town about ten miles away, and I knew exactly which shop Trevor was talking about. I'd been there once with Kaz when he'd needed a new copy of some old doo-wop record for his vinyl collection.

"I wish I could go with them," I said. "That place is kind of fun." I frowned as I took my phone back and scanned the text again. "I wish he'd at least invited me to go with them."

Vanessa looked sympathetic. "He probably didn't think about it, since he knew you had school."

I just nodded, not bothering to point out that the record shop was open late. He could have waited until *after* school. . . .

Okay, I knew I shouldn't have been so ridiculously disappointed. But could you blame me? I'd had such a great time with Trevor over the weekend, and I wanted to spend every moment possible with him while he was around. Still, he had to spend time with his family, too. That was why he was back, right? Besides, it was just one day.

Kaz bounded out of the classroom and almost crashed into us. "What are you two doing standing around out here?" he said. "Race you to the caf—I'm starving!"

"Yeah, me too." I shoved my phone back into my pocket. "Let's eat!"

I checked my watch for the ninth or tenth time. It was Tuesday afternoon, school had let out half an hour earlier, and all the buses were long gone. Aside from a few skateboarders practicing tricks over near the flagpole, I had the pickup area outside the main doors to myself.

"Where the heck are you, Trevor?" I muttered, pulling out my phone to make sure I hadn't missed a text.

When I looked up again, I finally saw Jon's low-slung old car peeling into the parking lot. He barely paused long enough for Trevor to hop out, grab his guitar off the seat, and slam the door shut before taking off again in a cloud of stinky exhaust. Waving my hand in front of my face to dissipate the smell, I hurried forward.

"Hey," I said, smiling. "I thought you'd never get here!"

He squinted at me. "Sorry. Jon wanted to stop off for tacos on the way."

"Oh." So much for my idea of going somewhere for a snack. "Okay. I'm glad you're here now, though."

"Me too." He smiled. "So what do you want to do?"

"I could give you that town tour," I said. "Give you a taste of my fabulous, exciting hometown?"

"Um, sure." He looked less than thrilled by the idea.

"Or we could hang out at the park?" I said quickly. "It's pretty nice there."

"Park sounds good." Trevor shrugged his guitar around behind his back on its long strap. "Lead the way."

Soon we were stepping through the scrolled iron gates of the park. For such a small town, its park was pretty large and fancy. There was a pond with ducks and swans and stuff, a big grass meadow where people could have picnics or play Frisbee, some wooded areas and flower gardens, and a gravel trail that made a loop through the whole thing.

We walked along for a while, not talking much, but just kind of comfortable together. When we passed a bench, Trevor paused.

"Want to sit for a minute?" he said. "Watch the ducks?"

"Sure." I sat down, glancing out across the pond, which shimmered in the afternoon sunshine. "This is nice, isn't it?"

"Yeah." Trevor settled his guitar on his lap, gazing out at the water. Then he glanced down at the guitar, adjusting it slightly and then strumming a chord.

"Are you getting bored?" I asked. "We could go do something else."

"Actually, I'm loving the peace and quiet." He grimaced. "Trust me, I'm not getting much of that while I'm staying with my relatives. I swear, my cousin's kid never shuts up."

"Reminds me of my brother," I said. "My parents say he was born talking." I paused. "Actually, they say the same thing about me, come to think of it."

He laughed. "You're a riot, Chloe! But listen, mind if I work on something for a sec? I had some ideas for one of our new songs, but I haven't had a chance to try them out yet. At least not when I could hear myself think, let alone play."

"Sure!" I was thrilled at the idea of watching him create a new hit for Of Note. "I'd love to hear that."

"Cool." He strummed a few more chords, humming under his

breath. Then he started picking out a tune, occasionally singing a word or two.

I sat back, enjoying the feel of the light afternoon breeze on my face as I listened. This was exactly the kind of thing I'd pictured when fantasizing about dating a rock god. Hanging out and listening to him play. Being part of the creative process. Maybe someday a reporter would interview me about this very moment, ask me to talk about how it had felt to be there at the inception of a classic hit. I tried to focus on every detail so I'd be sure to remember—just in case.

But after a few minutes my mind started to wander a little. I couldn't help it. Whatever Trevor was working on might be a classic hit someday, but right now it was just a bunch of random-sounding chord progressions.

A couple in their early twenties strolled past, hand in hand. The guy shot a curious look at both of us, while the girl was pretty much looking only at Trevor—obviously checking him out, even though he was at least five years younger. Not that I blamed her. He looked focused and serious and totally hot as he sat there bent over his guitar.

The pair moved on, disappearing around the next curve of the path. I wasn't sure Trevor had even noticed them.

"That sounds good," I said, trying to focus on the music again.

"Huh?" He looked up, blinking at me. "What did you say?"

I shook my head and smiled. "Nothing. Never mind. Sorry—keep going."

He nodded and went back to work.

• • •

Almost an hour later my mind had wandered so far, I wasn't sure it was even in the same zip code anymore. I mean, Trevor's playing was still amazing. But he'd barely looked up from his guitar in, like, twenty minutes, and I was getting a little bored.

Maybe that made me a bad rock-star girlfriend. Or just kind of distractible, like my teachers seemed to think. But I wasn't sure I could sit there much longer doing nothing. Not even with Trevor sitting beside me.

So maybe it was time to remind him I was there—maybe mix things up a little. Have some fun.

"Hey." I leaned closer and poked him in the arm. "Tag—you're it!"

Leaping to my feet, I took off toward the edge of the pond. But when I looked back, he was still sitting there, staring at me in confusion.

I jogged over to him. "I said tag, you're it," I said. "Come on. Catch me if you can. Betcha can't!"

He sighed and pushed his hair out of his eyes. "Did I miss something, Chloe? I thought we were having a nice time."

"We were." I flopped down beside him again. "I mean, we are. I was just thinking we could, you know, maybe walk around a little more. Or something."

"Oh." He glanced at his guitar and then up at me again. "Okay, can you give me another two seconds, though? I almost have this part worked out. Then we can do whatever you want, okay?"

"Okay. Sure. No problem." I collapsed back onto the bench, swallowing another sigh. Somehow, hanging out at the park with Trevor wasn't turning out to be quite as romantic as I'd expected. I drummed my fingers lightly on the bench beside me as I waited for him to finish.

And waited. And waited some more.

Ten minutes later I couldn't take it anymore. He was playing a sort of somber-sounding little riff. Taking a deep breath, I belted out a few cheerful la-la-la notes.

He jumped and then looked up at me again. "Chloe . . . ," he began.

"Sorry." I grinned weakly. "Just trying to help."

He frowned slightly and then sighed. "Sorry, I'm doing it again, aren't I?"

"Doing what?"

"Getting all obsessive." He flicked his hair back and smiled ruefully. "I tend to kind of forget everything else when I'm in the zone, you know?"

"It's okay," I said quickly. "That's one of the things I always liked about you. You know—even back at camp." I grinned. "Remember the time you were trying to learn that Mozart concerto on the violin?"

"It was Brahms, actually—the *Violin Concerto in D Major*," he corrected. "Yeah, I remember. You eventually hid my bow so I had to come play softball with the rest of you guys."

I laughed at the memory. "Too bad I forgot you had a spare

bow in your suitcase. We totally would've won that game if you'd stayed on second base where you belonged!"

Trevor chuckled. Then he plucked a string and hummed along with the note.

"Chloe, Chloe, Chloe," he sang softly, strumming the already familiar chords of "my" song. "You're the girl for me. . . ."

Suddenly I wasn't bored at all. I leaned a little closer, drinking in the sight of his earnest green eyes, the scent of the trees and the grass and the pond—and of course the sweet, sweet sound of the greatest guy in the world playing just for me.

"Ta-da!" I swung open the door of Aesop's Diner and led the way inside. "Here we are!"

Kaz, Vanessa, and Trevor were right behind me. That's right, I said Trevor. When we'd parted ways on Tuesday afternoon, I'd convinced him to join me and my friends at our favorite hang-out spot on Thursday after school. Okay, actually, I'd wanted to make it Wednesday. But Trevor's aunt and uncle had some sort of big family dinner planned on Wednesday, so Thursday it was.

Anyway, I figured this was his big chance to get to know my best friends. Sure, they'd met briefly at the marathon. But we'd been so busy, and Trevor had left so abruptly, there hadn't been much time for any serious bonding.

But here at the diner there would be no distractions. He would be able to get a big, juicy taste of my daily life. Not to mention some tasty Aesop's deliciousness.

One of the usual waitresses noticed us and waved us vaguely in the direction of our booth. Kaz charged over there.

"Hurry up, you guys. I'm famished," he said. "I just hope we don't end up with, like, steamed carrots and gluten-free pudding today."

Trevor gave him a strange look as he slid in beside me. "What's he talking about?"

"You'll see." I winked at my friends. "We have sort of a tradition about how we decide what to order."

He looked confused, but shrugged and reached for the water glass our waitress had just thunked down in front of him. "Be right back with menus," she told us.

As she hurried off, Kaz sat back and gazed at Trevor. "So," Kaz said. "You and Chloe, huh? What do you think of our girl?"

Trevor looked a little uncomfortable as he shot me a look. "Um . . ."

"Shut up, Kaz." I leaned across the table to smack him, though he easily dodged me. Then I gave Trevor an apologetic nudge with one shoulder. "Don't pay any attention to him. He's a wack job."

Vanessa giggled. "Yeah, Kaz is a nut." She nudged him with her shoulder. I couldn't help noticing they were sitting pretty close together.

"Okay." Trevor fiddled with his napkin. "So, uh, what do you guys do for fun around here?"

"This, mostly." Kaz waved a hand to indicate the diner. "Hang out. Play music. Achieve world peace. The usual."

"If you want fun, you should've been there for our jam at Kaz's birthday party," I told Trevor, grinning. "Did I tell you about that?"

"It was great," Vanessa agreed. "We had a serious jam session." She glanced at Trevor and blushed. "Probably not the same kind you'd have with your band, though."

"Cool." Trevor smiled. "Actually, my band loves to jam. We've come up with some of our best stuff that way over the years. Especially lately—we have this new drummer, okay? So one day last week we're taking a break, and she just starts waling on her kit, thump, thump, thump . . ." He banged on the table to illustrate, making our silverware jump. "I reacted first—I ran over and grabbed my axe, just started riffing to the beat. The other guys jumped in after a few seconds. We must have played for, like, half an hour like that." He smiled and stared into space, practically glowing with the memory.

I caught Kaz and Vanessa trading a look. "Um, cool, sounds very Dead of you guys," Kaz said.

Trevor blinked, returning to the here and now. "Did you say dead? What is that, local slang or something?"

"No, like the Grateful Dead," Kaz explained. "They're this old band that was famous for their long jams, and—"

"Yeah, I know who they were," Trevor cut in with a shrug. "My uncle used to follow them around in high school. He still has all these lame old bootlegs he's always trying to get me to listen to."

"Kaz loves all those lame old geezer bands," I put in. "He's always trying to get us to listen to them too. Right, Van?"

Vanessa nodded. "Look, she's finally bringing us a menu."

Sure enough, the waitress raced past, flinging a stack of menus onto our table without even slowing down.

"Nice service in this place," Trevor commented with more than a hint of sarcasm.

Kaz was already spreading one of the menus out in the middle of the table, tucking the extras away behind the napkin dispenser.

"Hey, can I have one of those?" Trevor said, reaching toward them.

"You won't need it," I said with a smile. "Check it out. We have this game we always play here—let's show him, guys."

"Me first." Kaz closed his eyes and held his finger a few inches above the menu. "Count me down, Chloe."

"Okay." I started the menu spinning. "Round and round she goes, where she stops . . ."

"Nobody knows!" Kaz sang out, punching his finger at the menu.

Vanessa leaned forward. "Bean burrito," she said. "Cool."

"Yeah, I guess." Kaz shrugged. "I could go for a burger, though. Why don't you see if you can get us one, Trevor?"

Trevor looked confused. "What do you mean? If you want a burger, just order a burger, right?"

"No, see, that's the game," I explained. "We can only order stuff we pick that way." I waggled my fingers at the menu. "Randomly, you know?"

He blinked at me. "Huh? Why?"

"Why not?" I was a little surprised by his reaction. My friends and I had loved our game from the first time Kaz had come up with the idea back in seventh grade. "It's more fun this way, right?"

He looked dubious. "Well, you guys can do what you want," he said. "I think I'll just order the normal way if that's okay with you all."

Once again, I saw Kaz and Van glance at each other. I just smiled weakly at Trevor. "Sure. Whatever."

My friends and I finished our game, ending up with a toasted bagel and some creamed corn to go with our burrito. But my heart wasn't in it the way it usually was.

Things didn't get much better after that, either. I couldn't help noticing Trevor wasn't really hitting it off with my friends. Oh, they were all being polite enough. They just didn't seem to have much in common. You know, other than me. And being music lovers, of course. Just maybe not the same kind . . .

Trevor had barely finished chewing the last bite of his grilled cheese sandwich when he glanced at his watch. "Jon will be picking me up soon," he told me. "I should get going."

"What? Already?" I exclaimed.

"I told him to meet me at your place," he added. "Figured I'd walk you home. You know, wait for him there."

"Oh." Now I felt much less disappointed. Maybe he hadn't clicked with my friends yet. But Trevor and I always clicked just fine when we were alone. My mind flashed to that almost-kiss the last time he'd walked me to my door, and I smiled. "Okay, let's go. Later, guys."

My friends mumbled good-byes as Trevor and I left. As soon as we were outside, he took my hand.

"That's more like it." He smiled down at me. "Your friends are nice and all. But it's awesome to hang out with you—you know, just the two of us."

I squeezed his hand. "Yeah, I know what you mean," I said as we strolled down the block, hand in hand. "Maybe we can get together tomorrow? I mean, you already told me your reunion is on Saturday, right? So tomorrow after school will be our last chance to get together before the dance, and—"

"Okay, okay!" He laughed, squeezing my hand. "You don't have to try to talk me into hanging out with you again, Chloe. Tomorrow sounds great."

"Great." I smiled sheepishly. "Sorry. Guess I'm just anxious to get in as much time together as we can. I mean, it feels like you just got here and you're leaving in, like, three days. . . ."

"Chill," he said. "It's cool."

"Okay." I wasn't sure I liked him telling me to chill when I was just trying to have a conversation. But when I looked up at him, he was smiling down at me again.

"Chloe, Chloe, Chloe, you're the girl for me," he sang softly, his voice husky and low. "Zoe, Zoe, Zoe, you're all I see. . . ."

I froze. "Hey," I said. "Did you just sing the wrong girl's name right there?"

Trevor looked startled. But then he laughed and shook his head.

"Oh man," he said. "Sorry, Chloe, guess I'm getting even less sleep than I thought! My little cousin kept the whole house up for hours last night screaming his lousy little head off." He ran his free hand through his hair. "Anyway, I guess Zoe's name is on my brain too—the whole band's really psyched about her. You know, what her drumming adds to our sound?"

"Oh." I bit my lip, still not sure how to feel about the slip. Yeah, he'd been talking about Zoe a lot. That was only natural—he talked about all his bandmates a lot. But accidentally slipping her name into *my* song?

Trevor dropped my hand and slid his arm around my shoulders, squeezing me up against his side. "Forgive me?" he whispered.

I shivered, loving the feel of his arm around me. So what if he'd messed up our names? They did sound pretty similar, and he was only human, right?

"Of course," I said, snuggling against him. "No biggie."

All too soon we reached my house. On the porch, he finally let go of me and turned so we were face-to-face. "Okay," he said. "I guess I'll see you tomorrow, right?"

"Right." I held my breath, waiting to see what happened next.

He leaned a little closer, suddenly looking nervous. Adorable! As gorgeous as he was, somehow I'd figured he'd be totally smooth when it came to stuff like this.

"Wait," I said, a little breathless as I saw his lips come even closer to mine. "Have you ever—"

Bang!

The front door flew open, and my little brother blasted out, almost running into us. "Out of my way," he said, darting between us. "I need to get the mail."

As Timothy hurried toward the mailbox, Trevor stepped back. "Okay, see you," he blurted out, his face going red. "I'll go wait for Jon by the road."

"I—um . . . ," I began helplessly.

But it was no use. The moment was gone—ruined by my total dork of a brother.

Oh well. Maybe this was fate. Maybe we were supposed to share our first kiss during a more romantic moment than on some random Thursday afternoon.

I smiled, liking that idea. After all, it just gave me one more thing to look forward to at the dance.

Chapter Fifteen

On Friday at school, I sat at lunch listening to Kaz and Vanessa plan their outfits for their big date to the dance the next night. Most people would just be wearing regular fancy dress-up clothes, but my friends and I always preferred to liven things up by inventing our own themes. This time they'd decided to go with a *Great Gatsby* theme, since we'd read the book earlier that semester. I wasn't sure exactly when they'd come up with the idea, which once again made me feel like the third wheel on a bicycle. Normally we always planned stuff like that together—the three of us.

But I've been spending a lot of my free time with Trevor lately, I reminded myself, sipping my water as Vanessa laughed over Kaz's idea to switch roles and have him dress as Daisy and her as Gatsby. No wonder they didn't want to wait for my opinion.

Besides, this time it wasn't about the three of us—it was about the two of them. As a couple.

As usual, thinking about that made me feel strange. For a second I almost wished Trevor hadn't come to town. That way we'd all be going to the dance together, the three of us, just like always. We'd all be planning our outfits together, just like always. Having a great time together, just like always.

Or maybe I'd be Kaz's date, a little voice in my head piped in.

I banished that insane little voice immediately. Yes, Kaz had asked me to the dance. But that was over, and now he was into Vanessa—just as I'd hoped.

Anyway, I needed to get a grip. Kaz was my friend—that was all. And yes, I always had fun goofing around with my friends, but I could hang out with them anytime. A date with Trevor, on the other hand? That could be a once-in-a-lifetime romantic moment, one I'd savor forever.

Just then Vanessa turned to me. "So, Chloe," she said, "your next big date with Trevor is today, right? What are you guys going to do?"

"Make-Out Point?" Kaz guessed. "Vegas wedding? Whirlwind trip to Paris?"

I rolled my eyes at him. "Actually, I was thinking we'd go catch the instrument thing at the museum."

Kaz's eyes lit up with interest. "I almost forgot about that." He glanced at Vanessa. "Maybe we should try to go too."

"Sure," she said. "But we're not going today. No way are we going to risk barging in on Chloe's date."

Kaz grinned. "You're no fun."

Vanessa giggled. I smiled, but thinking of the two of them going to that exhibit without me made me feel squirmy and empty.

Still, I supposed I'd have to get used to that feeling. If Kaz and Van were going to be a couple now, like Trevor and I, there would probably be plenty of other times they did stuff without me. Private jokes shared just by the two of them. Dinner dates and dances and all the rest.

I wasn't sure I liked that idea. But if it made them happy, I'd be happy for them. It was too late to turn back now.

When I emerged from school, Trevor was leaning against the wall, watching the skate rats do their thing. He hurried over as soon as he saw me coming.

"Hey," he said, smiling at me and then nodding at Kaz and Vanessa, who were right behind me. "Oh, hi," he said to them. "Are you guys, um, coming with us?"

"Nope. She's all yours," Vanessa said with a shy smile. "We were just walking her out."

"Make sure you have her home by midnight or she'll turn into a pumpkin," Kaz added.

"Go." I gave him a playful shove, eager to be alone with Trevor. "Text you later."

"Have fun." Vanessa started dragging Kaz off toward the buses.

"Don't do anything I wouldn't do, kids!" Kaz called back.

I ignored him, smiling up at Trevor. "Ready to go?"

"Sure." He took my hand. "Where are we going?"

"I was thinking we could go check out that exhibit," I said. "Remember? The one I told you about the other day?"

He looked blank. "Refresh my memory?"

"Antique musical instruments," I said. "At the local museum? It's supposed to be really interesting."

"Hmm." He ran his thumb over the back of my hand and then shrugged. "Sounds cool, but I'm not sure I'm in the mood today. I was thinking maybe we could hang out at the park again instead."

"The park?" I bit my lip. "Um . . ."

"Is that okay?" He spun me around to face him. "I mean, if you had your heart set on the museum thing . . ."

"No, it's fine," I said quickly. "Let's go to the park."

I was a little disappointed, since I'd been looking forward to the exhibit. But what was the big deal? I could catch the exhibit later with Kaz and Vanessa. Or, well, if they'd already gone together, I was sure I could find someone else to go with. . . .

I tried not to worry about it, focusing instead on the feel of Trevor's warm hand in mine. He asked me about my day, and I filled him in on the boring details as we made the short five-block walk to the park.

Soon we were back on our same bench. Trevor had a packet of crackers in his pocket and we fed the crackers to the ducks. Then we settled back and started talking about music.

Well, actually, Trevor did most of the talking. He was full

of plans and dreams for his band. Starting with lots of gigs at that local club in his town, then maybe a write-up on some music blogs, and after that, who knew?

I was happy to discuss all the exciting possibilities with him. At least for the first half hour or so. But after a while, he was mostly just saying the same stuff over and over. Did he even realize it? I wasn't sure. Either way, I actually found myself getting a little bored. Again. Was that possible?

At first I told myself I was crazy. This was what I wanted, right? Lots of private time with Trevor, talking about the thing that had brought us together, obsessing together over our shared passion—music. So why wasn't I feeling it?

I had no idea, but I figured it wasn't Trevor's fault I seemed to be in a weird mood today. So I kept quiet, nodding and smiling at what I hoped were appropriate times.

A tinny little snippet of a recent dance hit snapped me out of it and interrupted whatever Trevor was saying. For a second I thought it was my phone, but it turned out to be his. "Hey, I use that ringtone for Vanessa," I said.

"Really? Cool." He glanced at the screen and then shot me a smile. "It's the band. I should probably take it in case it's important—be right back."

He hurried off, pressing the phone to his ear. I watched as he disappeared behind a tree. Then I leaned back against the hard, scratchy wood of the bench, wondering what exactly was wrong with me. Here I was on a totally romantic date with the hottest and most talented guy in the world. And I could barely stop myself from yawning in his face whenever he started getting all excited about the topic that had brought us together in the first place.

It was kind of ridiculous when I thought about it that way. How many other girls would love to be in my shoes right now?

I glanced around, realizing Trevor's phone call was taking an awfully long time. I was trying to decide whether to go over there to see if everything was okay when he finally reappeared.

"Hey," he said, hurrying toward me. "I got a text from Jon while I was on the phone. He's on his way to pick me up."

"Now?" I jumped to my feet, startling a squirrel that had been nosing around near the bench. "But I thought we were talking about getting some food, or—"

"Sorry." He reached out and squeezed my shoulder. "Jon's kind of a pain, so I didn't want to argue. If I want him to drive me over to that dance tomorrow night . . ."

"Okay, okay," I said hastily. I definitely didn't want to risk messing up our big romantic night. No matter how weird I was feeling today, I was still sure that was going to be an evening to remember. "A moment," like the song said. "Come on. I'll walk you out."

Jon turned up a few minutes later, barely sparing me a nod as he idled the car loudly at the curb. This time there wasn't even a hint of a good-bye kiss, which was fine with me. I could wait one more night.

When Trevor was gone, I wandered toward home, still thinking about my weird reaction to today's get-together. It already didn't seem quite real. I mean, how could I be bored when I was with Trevor? It just didn't compute.

My phone buzzed, snapping me out of it. It was a text from Kaz.

Hope I'm not interrupting your big date. Just wanted to see how the exhibit was. I'm psyched to see it soon, so give me a review ASAP!

I hesitated and then clicked off the phone without responding. For some reason I wasn't ready to tell him we hadn't gone to that exhibit after all. Why? I had no idea, but it wasn't a big deal. I'd fill my friends in on everything soon—just not right that minute.

No biggie.

Chapter Sixteen

I awoke to the sound of a gobbling turkey on Saturday morning. "Urgh," I mumbled, rolling over and scrabbling for my phone.

The text from Kaz was short: *Aesop's 10 a.m.*

Rubbing the sleep from my eyes, I sat up and texted him back, saying I'd be there. Then I stretched and glanced at the window to see what the weather was like.

As I did, I noticed the cute red dress hanging on the back of my door. That woke me up the rest of the way. I sat up and stared at the dress, trying to feel as psyched about tonight's big dance as I knew I should. Because this was what I'd been waiting for, dreaming about. Right? True romance.

"Definitely," I said, deciding to be positive about all this. Yesterday had been an aberration. Just a combination of a weird mood and Jon's usual bad timing. No biggie.

At exactly ten a.m. I stepped into the diner. Kaz and Vanessa were already at our table. Once again they were sitting on the same side of the booth. Cute.

"Look at you two, all early and stuff," I commented as I reached them.

Kaz glanced up from turning his straw wrapper into a weird little snake. "You're just in time. We were about to go ahead and order without you."

"No, we weren't." Vanessa smiled. "Hurry up and sit down, though. We're dying to hear about your date with Trevor yesterday!"

"Yeah, it must've been pretty great since you never bothered to text me back," Kaz put in.

"Leave her alone," Vanessa said with a giggle. "She's twitterpated, remember?"

I made a face at her. "Stop."

"Okay, we don't need any gory details about dreamy rock star Trevor." Kaz fluttered his eyelashes dramatically, making a weird face I guessed was supposed to represent my feelings for Trevor. Or maybe his feelings about my feelings. Whatever. "Just tell us about the exhibit. Worth going?"

"Um . . ." I shrugged. "Actually, we didn't end up doing that."

"Really?" Vanessa looked surprised. "How come? It seemed like something Trevor would really like. I mean, he's so into music and all, right?"

"Yeah, I know. I thought so too." I shrugged again. "Guess he just wasn't in a museum mood."

"Oh. That's too bad." Vanessa shot Kaz a quick look. He raised an eyebrow in response, though he didn't say a word.

Just then a waitress bustled over and tossed some menus at us. "Anything to drink?" she asked, sounding bored.

"Iced tea, please," I said.

The others ordered their drinks too. As the waitress hurried off, Kaz grabbed a menu.

"Ready to figure out our order?" he asked.

Okay, I guessed that meant he didn't want to talk about Trevor anymore. Fine by me.

"My turn to go first," I said, lifting a finger in preparation. "Spin me, someone."

We spent the next few minutes playing the menu game. My finger landed on the chocolate milkshake, which we all agreed was a fine choice for breakfast. Then Kaz got us a pastrami wrap, and Vanessa added fried calamari to the list. We decided we were all hungry enough to go for one more item, and this time Kaz's finger pointed to Belgian waffles with Canadian bacon.

"Very international," I commented. "Also appropriately breakfasty, so score."

"We need to carbo-load, right?" Vanessa said with a smile. "For all that dancing tonight."

"Right." Kaz did a little shimmy right there in the booth.

"After we eat, I've got to go home and dust off my boogie shoes."

"Great. While you're doing that, maybe Vanessa can come over and we can get ready together." I tilted my head and shot her my best smile. "What do you say, up for more primping?"

"Definitely," she said immediately. "It'll be fun."

"Hold on." Kaz sat up straight, looking interested. "My boogie shoes aren't all that dusty. I could probably find the time to come over too."

"No way." Vanessa giggled and winked at me. "No boys allowed! We need our girly time, right, Chloe?"

"Right." I was relieved she'd said that. Somehow I'd sort of forgotten the three of us normally did get ready for stuff like this together. But tonight? It would have been totally awkward primping and prettying myself up for Trevor with Kaz right there. "You shouldn't see your date before it's time to go to the dance, anyway. It's bad luck."

"Isn't that only for weddings?" Vanessa said. Then, apparently realizing what she'd just said, she blushed deep red. "And we're definitely not—I mean, you know . . ."

"Excuse me," Kaz said, sliding out of the booth. "Be right back—I need to hit the head."

He scurried off in the direction of the restroom. I grinned at Van.

"What do you know?" I said. "Apparently, it actually is possible to embarrass Mr. Kazuo Aratani!"

Her face was still red, but she laughed. "Do I get an award?"

"I think you should. I only wish I'd been filming, since nobody would ever believe it happened."

She looked alarmed at that. "You're not going to tell anyone?" she exclaimed. "I mean, you know Kaz and I aren't—That is, we don't really—"

"Relax, I won't say a word." I twiddled my fork, hoping our food came soon. All I'd had for breakfast back at home had been a glass of OJ.

She shot me a sidelong look. "Are you okay? You seemed kind of—I don't know, down or something when you got here."

"Actually"—I glanced in the direction of the restroom to make sure Kaz had really left—"you're kind of right. Yesterday, well . . ."

"What?" she prompted, her eyes soft and concerned.

I shrugged, still playing with the fork. "I guess hanging out with Trevor this week hasn't always been quite as nonstop perfect as I thought it would be, you know?"

"Really?" She looked surprised. "But I thought he keeps holding your hand and stuff, and then he wrote you that song. . . ."

"I know, I know." I sighed and dropped the fork. "But the thing is, we spend pretty much all our time talking about his band. Which was fine at first, but I guess it would be nice if he seemed interested in anything else, you know? Maybe wanted to talk about me once in a while, or really anything but . . ."

Vanessa cleared her throat loudly, tilting her head to the side. Looking that way, I saw Kaz returning.

"Maybe we can talk about it later," she said quietly.

I nodded as Kaz reached us. It was probably just as well we'd been cut off. There was really nothing to talk about; it was just me being weird and looking for trouble. After all, nobody had ever said love was easy. Especially when it was mostly long distance, and we had to pack several months' worth of true romance into a week.

But that was okay. Trevor was worth it. I was still sure of that.

My parents and Timothy were just leaving as Vanessa arrived that afternoon.

"Hi, Bells," Vanessa said. "Bye, Bells."

My mother chuckled. "Be good, you two," she said, pulling on her jacket. "We'll be home late."

"Which means you'd better be home before us," my dad added with a wink.

"Unless you're in jail," Timothy said. "Then we'll bail you out in the morning."

"Hardy har, you're a laugh riot." I gave him a little shove, and he kicked me in the shin before darting outside.

"Where are they off to?" Vanessa asked as the door shut behind my family.

"Movies," I said. "Timothy finally talked them into taking him to some dumb double-feature monster film festival over on the other side of Smithton."

"Sounds kind of fun, actually," Vanessa said. "Kaz would probably love to go next time."

I smirked. "Look at you, thinking of more stuff to do with Kaz now that you're officially dating at all."

She blushed. "No, we're not," she said. "We're just going to this dance together, that's all. And only because you're ditching us for Mr. Perfect."

"You sure about that?" I'd meant the question to come out light and funny, but it ended up a little more intense than that.

Vanessa shot me a surprised look. Then she took a deep breath, and her mouth stretched into a shy smile. "Well, actually . . . ," she began.

"What?" I leaned forward, suddenly nervous. "Actually what?"

She shrugged. "I guess we can just see what happens," she said, looking down and fiddling with her makeup bag so I couldn't see her eyes. "For now let's just say this is definitely a date, okay?"

"Okay." I wasn't sure what else to say, especially since I couldn't quite read the expression on her face for once. What was she thinking?

I decided not to worry about it. "Come on. Let's get gussied up for our fellas," I said, grinning. "Last one upstairs has to deal with my hair!"

Soon we were dressed in fuzzy robes and sitting in front of the big full-length mirror in my bathroom. Vanessa started working on my hair, smoothing its wild curls into soft ringlets.

"So what did you and Kaz decide to wear in the end?" I asked, realizing I'd never heard the result of their discussions.

"Still *Great Gatsby*," she mumbled around the bobby pins in her mouth. "But I vetoed the cross-dressing thing. Not that it wouldn't be funny. I just don't want him wrecking my flapper dress."

I laughed, picturing Kaz, limbs and fringe flailing on the dance floor. "Good call," I said. "Besides, you look superhot in that dress. I'm glad you're wearing it again."

"I know I just wore it at the marathon." She shrugged. "But I like it."

I smiled at her in the mirror. That was my Vanessa—some girls might be self-conscious about wearing the same dress to back-to-back events. But not her. She marched to her own drummer. We all did, really. That was part of why we got along so well.

"Who else would have us?" I murmured with a smile.

"Huh?" Vanessa looked up from my hair.

"Nothing. Hurry up and finish so I can do your hair next." I smiled at her again. "I want to have lots of time to take pictures before the boys get here."

An hour and a half later we both looked fabulous. I'd teased Vanessa's blond hair into an elaborate twist on top of her head, which made her look older and intriguingly exotic. She'd made my curls look like they were there on purpose. Our makeup matched our looks—mine modern and rock 'n' roll, hers with the bold drama of the Roaring Twenties.

"We are so hot," I declared, snapping another selfie of the two of us in my front hall.

Her phone buzzed. "It's Kaz," she said, scanning the text. "He says he's already dressed and could come over a little early if we asked him nicely."

I laughed. Kaz had already called once and texted twice, but we'd declined all his requests to come over early. No boys allowed!

"Tell him he can make it another fifteen minutes or so," I said. "By then it'll be time for him to come pick us up anyway." Realizing what I'd just said, I shook my head and corrected myself. "I mean, pick *you* up."

I'd exchanged a few quick texts with Trevor earlier, arranging for him to come to get me. With Jon as chauffeur, of course. I wasn't super-pumped about arriving at the dance in his smelly old car, but whatever. At least I'd be arriving with Trevor. That was the important part.

"*You'll know it's true on a magical night*," I sang.

Vanessa joined in for the rest: "*Whether sailing at sea or dancing in the moonlight. That's when you'll share a first kiss if you dare. Remember it always: true romance is rare.*"

I grabbed the hairbrush out of Vanessa's hand and used it as a microphone as we belted out the chorus:

"*True romance. It's the air that we breathe. Just us two together. Yeah, just you and me!*"

Vanessa started giggling then, and we collapsed against each other, laughing so hard, we couldn't breath. Finally I pulled back, tweaking a stray bit of hair back into her updo.

"This was fun," I said. "Getting ready, you know."

"I know." She smiled at me. "Come on. Let's go take more pictures outside while we wait for the guys. They'll be here pretty soon."

I shivered with anticipation. Now that it was almost time for the dance, my earlier worries seemed silly. This was going to be a fabulous night—one Trevor and I would probably talk about for the rest of our lives. I couldn't wait for it to start.

I grabbed my phone and my purse and headed for the door. "Let's go!"

Chapter Seventeen

Vanessa and I had fun for the next few minutes striking silly poses and snapping tons of photos and a couple of videos. If any of my neighbors happened to be looking out their windows, they probably thought we were insane. Finally I tucked my phone into my purse.

"Enough," I said, still snorting with laughter. "I don't want to totally run down my battery before the dance even starts."

"Okay." She put her phone away too. Then we settled ourselves carefully on the front porch steps to wait for our dates.

After a moment of silence I looked over at her, wanting to ask how she felt about going to the dance with Kaz. Was she excited? Nervous? Did she think there was a chance they'd become an actual couple?

For some reason, though, I wasn't sure I was ready to hear the answer to that last part, especially after the way she'd acted earlier. So I kept quiet, and she was the first to speak.

"I wonder what everyone at school will think of Trevor," she said, giving me a sidelong smile.

I shrugged, playing with the hem of my dress. "A lot of them have already seen him," I reminded her. "At the marathon, remember?"

"Oh right. I guess his guitar solo was kind of, um, memorable." She giggled.

"True." I went a little starry-eyed at the memory. "I just wish he'd been there when we played 'True Romance.' That would've been epic!"

Vanessa nodded. "Do you think the DJ will play that song tonight?"

Before I could answer, there was a weird honking sound from the end of the block. It sounded like a goose with emphysema.

Jumping to my feet, I peered in that direction. "Whoa, what is *that*?" I exclaimed.

A car was coming our way. It was one of those old-timey antique ones, with a bright yellow body and a black hardtop and funny bicyclelike tires.

It honked again and then pulled to a stop in front of my house. With a flourish, Kaz jumped out of the passenger seat.

"Your chariot awaits, milady!" he called, striding up to Vanessa and sweeping into a deep bow.

"Wow." I stared at the car idling loudly at the curb. "Where'd you come up with that thing, Kaz?"

He grinned, looking pleased with himself. "It's the closest I could come to a *Gatsby* car," he said. "I mean, it's yellow instead of cream colored, and it's not technically an actual Rolls-Royce, but . . ."

"It's amazing!" Vanessa said with a giggle, waving to the man in the driver's seat, who tipped his hat to her. Yes, he was wearing an actual hat—one as old-fashioned as the car, and pretty similar to the one Kaz had paired with his own dapper *Gatsby* suit. Which he looked pretty great in, by the way.

"Who's that?" I asked, giving the driver a wave myself.

"His daughter is one of my dad's patients," Kaz said. "When he heard about our outfits, he offered to play chauffeur."

I wasn't surprised. Kaz was that kind of person—everyone loved being part of his schemes, since they were usually a lot of fun. Just look at the dance marathon, for instance. The whole school—the whole town, really—was still buzzing about what a blast it had been. And it had all started with Kaz, like most of the fun stuff around here.

Vanessa laughed again, looking a little breathless and pink cheeked. "I guess we shouldn't keep our chauffeur waiting."

"Right. Sorry I was a little late, but I figured you wouldn't mind when you got a load of our ride." Kaz gallantly offered his arm. "Shall we depart?"

Kaz's mention of being late reminded me to check my watch. He was right—it was almost ten minutes after the time we'd told both guys to pick us up. So where was Trevor?

Vanessa seemed to be thinking the same thing. "Want to ride with us, Chloe?" she asked. "You could text Trevor to tell him you'll meet him at the dance."

I hesitated, tempted by the offer. It would be a blast to show up at the dance in that car with my two best friends. Just like old times.

But this wasn't old times. Things were different now. Trevor was expecting to take me to the dance. And besides, I shouldn't horn in on Kaz and Vanessa's first real date. Not if they were going to have a chance to really see if they wanted to be together.

"It's okay," I said, ignoring the unpleasant little twist in my gut at the last part. "I'm sure he'll be here soon." I pulled out my phone to double-check for texts. "He's coming straight from his family reunion, so he's probably just a little behind."

"Rock 'n' roll time, right?" Kaz winked and grinned. "Sure you don't want to catch a ride with us? It's not every day you get to ride in one of these babies." He gestured toward the antique car, then turned and smiled at me.

That smile. It was killing me tonight for some reason, even though I'd seen it a zillion times before. How lucky was I to even know a guy like Kaz? Suddenly I was afraid I might start bawling right then and there. Which was weird, since I hardly ever cry.

Then again this was a special night. I was probably just letting my excitement over the big date with Trevor get to me. Or maybe I was getting emotional at the thought that my two best friends might fall in love tonight. That would be enough to make anyone a little weepy, right?

"Thanks," I said. "You two, go ahead. I'll see you there in a bit."

"Okay." Vanessa gave me a quick hug and then stuck her arm through Kaz's. "Shall we depart, sir?"

"Indeed, madam."

That little gut twist hit me again. They were so cute together. But it still bothered me to think of things changing. Of the two of them having secrets I wasn't part of.

Get over it, I told myself. *Things change. That's life. You should be happy for them.*

And I was. Except . . .

I watched with a forced smile as the two of them marched over to the car. When they got closer, the driver hopped out and opened the back door for them.

"Please, dude—allow me." Kaz took the door handle and ushered Vanessa into the backseat himself. His hand grazed her bare shoulder, and I shivered, almost able to feel the touch on my own skin. But I kept the smile on my face as Kaz tipped his hat to the driver and climbed in after Vanessa. The driver closed the door, then got back in and started the car.

I waved as they drove off in a cloud of fumes. There was one more goose honk, and then the yellow car disappeared around the corner, and I could finally relax.

What was wrong with me? This was supposed to be an exciting, romantic night for me and Trevor. So why was I suddenly obsessing over my friends' date instead of my own?

Maybe because it could have been me, I thought before I could stop myself. *I could be in that car right now instead of Vanessa.*

That thought made me feel like the worst, most hateful, and petty friend in the world. How could I be jealous of my two favorite people? It had been my idea for them to go to the dance together, and now here I was wishing I'd never mentioned it.

It was getting a little chilly, so I went back inside to wait for Trevor. The house was still and silent, which made my mood drop even further. Pulling out my phone, I brought up Trevor's band's version of "True Romance" and cranked up the volume, humming along.

But for once, the magic of the song didn't work. Every time I tried to picture myself slow dancing with Trevor, I kept imagining my arms holding someone else.

Kaz.

"Oh no!" I said aloud, my voice echoing through the quiet house. "I think I've made a huge mistake!"

My heart pounded as I tried to tell myself it was nerves talking or anticipation or just a plain old psychotic break.

But no. I couldn't deny the truth any longer. I was sitting here waiting for Trevor . . . and wishing I were with Kaz instead.

At that moment I heard a loud backfire from outside, and when I stepped to the window, Jon's car was pulling to the curb in front of my house.

I gulped. What in the world was I supposed to do now?

Chapter Eighteen

When I swung open the front door, Jon was right there. "Gotta use the john," he muttered with a scowl. "Where is it?"

"Uh, come right in." I stepped back to let him pass. "The bathroom's down that hall past the stairs."

His only response was a grunt as he took off in that direction. Trevor came in behind his cousin, looking apologetic.

"Sorry about Jon," he said. "He and his girlfriend had a huge fight on the phone right before we left the reunion. He's not in the best mood."

"I can tell." I tried to sound normal, but it wasn't easy. My mind was still spinning with the revelation that had just hit me. How was I supposed to act now that I knew I was going to the dance with the wrong guy?

Then again how could I do anything else? Trevor had come all the way here just for me. I couldn't just blow him off now.

Besides, there was no point thinking about what this night might have been like if I were with Kaz. Because he was at the dance with my other best friend. And I wasn't about to do anything to hurt Vanessa, especially if she was starting to have feelings for Kaz too. I wouldn't do that to her—to either of them.

You had your chance, that evil little voice inside of me piped up. *It could've been you. But you blew it.*

Good point, evil little voice. Taking a deep breath, I managed to shoot Trevor what I hoped was a pleasant and relatively sane smile. "Want to sit down while we wait for Jon?"

"Sure." He followed me into the living room. For the first time, I noticed he looked amazing in a dark suit jacket over jeans and a concert T-shirt. *Very rock 'n' roll,* Kaz might have said. For a second I felt a shiver of the old feelings creep back.

But that wasn't real. It was just a fantasy, like the song I'd thought was predicting my future. Kaz? Now that was real. Or it could be if it wasn't already too late.

"So," Trevor said after what I realized was an awkwardly long moment of silence. He was sitting on the edge of the sofa holding his cell phone, tossing it back and forth from one hand to the other. "This should be fun. The dance, I mean."

"Yeah." I glanced toward the hall, wishing Jon would hurry up.

Trevor seemed to be thinking the same thing. "I'll go see what's keeping him," he said. "Be right back."

Dropping his phone onto the coffee table, he took off. I leaned back in my chair, feeling oddly drained, even though the evening hadn't even started yet. How the heck was I going to pull this off? How was I going to smile and flirt and dance with Trevor, when all I could think about was Kaz?

Before I could figure it out, Trevor's phone rang. It only took a second to recognize the tune—a recent hit called "Fun Girl." Curious in spite of myself, I leaned forward so I could see the readout. It was a call from someone named Z.

Zoe, I realized. I glanced toward the hall, wondering if Trevor would want me to answer it. Before I could decide, he hurried in and grabbed the phone himself, glancing at the display.

"Zoe?" he said, answering. "Hang on a sec, okay?"

He lowered the phone and smiled at me. "Jon's on his phone in your bathroom," he said. "He's fighting with Shelly again, I think." He held up his own phone. "Mind if I take this while we wait?"

"Go ahead." I wandered out into the hall to give him some privacy. Twenty-four hours ago I probably would have been fighting back jealousy at a call from Zoe. And maybe I would have been right to feel that way. Because looking back, it was pretty obvious he thought she was something special. And maybe not just in a talented-drummer kind of way.

It was weird to realize I didn't care. So what if Trevor and Zoe liked each other? More power to them. Maybe they'd end up being the perfect couple.

Like me and Kaz . . .

Suddenly Trevor's voice grew loud enough to carry into the hallway. "I can't do it, seriously," he exclaimed. "I told you, she asked me to this, like, two weeks ago, and if I bag out now . . ." There was a pause. I crept closer to the doorway, unable to resist listening. "Look, don't be like that, Zoe," he said after a moment, his voice softening. "You know it's not like that. When I get back . . ." Another pause. "Look, I can't help it. I'm sure they'll want us again, right? Anyway, I have to go. I'll text you later."

I scooted across to the front door, pretending to be looking out the little window beside it when he emerged into the foyer. "Everything okay?" I asked.

"Sure." He looked troubled. "I mean, yeah, definitely. It turns out they want us at that club I was telling you about."

"The Scene?" I exclaimed. "Really? That's amazing, Trevor! Congratulations."

"Yeah." He didn't look happy. "The thing is, there was a cancellation tonight. They wanted us to step in for the ten-o'clock show."

"Tonight?"

"Uh-huh." He slumped against the wall, staring at his phone. "Talk about bad timing. . . ."

Yeah. Or was it?

"Hold on," I said. "Ten o'clock? But it's barely seven now."

"Yeah. So?" He shrugged.

"So you could still make it." Crossing the foyer in two big

strides, I grabbed his hand. "You can't pass up this break, Trev. And it sounds like Jon's not in the mood for the dance anyway. Why not see if he can run you back there right now?"

"What?" He stared at me, perplexed. "But your dance—I can't bail on you, Chloe. That wouldn't be cool."

"Who needs moonlight and red roses and fancy dinners anyway?" I said. "I'd rather just order random food at the diner with . . ."

My voice trailed off with a wince as I thought about Kaz. If Trevor hadn't come to town at just the right—or wrong?—time, I'd probably be at the dance with Kaz right now. And suddenly I knew that's what I really wanted. To be *with* Kaz.

Trevor furrowed his eyebrows, waiting for me to finish, but instead I quickly blurted out, "Seriously, I don't mind. This week has been fun, Trevor. It's been great getting to know you again after all these years, and I hope we'll totally stay friends from now on. But . . ."

"Hang on." He tilted his head, staring at me. "Are you . . . breaking up with me?"

"I don't know." I shrugged sheepishly. "Maybe. I mean, were we even officially going out?"

"I don't know." He looked more confused than ever. "I never really thought about it, I guess."

Typical guy, I thought with a tiny smile. "Well, I have," I told him. "And the thing is, I think we're better as friends. Especially since I think there might be someone else you like for real."

He frowned. "What are you talking about?"

"Zoe. Duh." I rolled my eyes. "Could you possibly talk about her even more, dude? Anyone can tell you're twitterpated."

"Twitter-what?" He was still frowning. "Anyway, Zoe and I are just friends. Nothing more."

"I know, I know, you keep telling me that." I poked him in the chest. "Face it, Trev. She's your Yoko."

He looked alarmed. "No way! I won't let this break up the band."

I laughed. "Way to be Mr. Literal. I just mean I think it makes more sense for you to be with someone, you know, in the same area code. And for me, too."

"Oh." He still looked wary for a second. Then his expression cleared. "Wait. Is this about that guy?"

"What guy?"

"Your buddy Kaz." He took a step closer. "I could tell he was into you."

"Maybe he used to be," I said softly, thinking about him and Vanessa at the dance. "I'm not so sure anymore." I forced a smile. "But never mind that—you'll need to hit the road now if you're going to make that show. I mean, I know it's totally rock 'n' roll to show up late, but there are limits."

He stared at me, his expression wavering between excitement and uncertainty. At that moment Jon crashed into the room.

"Women," he spat out. "They suck." Glancing at me, he added, "No offense."

"Does this mean you're not going to the dance?" I asked him.

He just shrugged. "I can still drop you two off, I guess," he muttered sourly.

I smiled at Trevor. "I have a better idea. . . ."

Five minutes later they were gone. Trevor had thanked me about eleventy zillion times in those five minutes, still seeming a little shell-shocked.

But he'd get over it by the time he made it back to his own town. I was sure of it. Would he and Zoe end up together? Yeah, I was pretty sure of that, too.

So where did that leave me?

Chapter Nineteen

I'm not sure how long I wandered around my house trying to figure out what to do next. Should I still go to the dance? It was tempting. But I didn't want to be at the center of some pity party.

Still, I couldn't just not show up, either. Digging my cell phone out of my purse, I clicked open a group text to Kaz and Vanessa.

Then I stopped, not sure what to say. Especially when I pictured Kaz—sweet, goofy Kaz—asking me to the dance. And playing the oboe outside my window. And grinning hopefully as he waited for me to break his heart.

With a grimace, I deleted the group text. Instead I started a text to just Vanessa.

Probably won't make the dance after all. Tell u more later. Have fun!

I added a smiley emoji at the end and then clicked send. Then

I waited, sure Vanessa would text back immediately with follow-up questions. But a minute or two passed, and my phone stayed silent.

Finally I shrugged and tossed the phone aside. Maybe Vanessa was having such a good time with Kaz that she'd turned off her phone. Or maybe it was sitting in her purse in a dark corner somewhere while the two of them danced the night away, wrapped in each other's arms. . . .

I squeezed my eyes shut, banishing the image. What was the point in torturing myself? Either Kaz and Vanessa would fall in love or they wouldn't. I wasn't going to interfere, even now that I'd finally woken up and realized Kaz and I had been the ones who were meant to be all along. If "meant to be" was even a thing, that is.

"Stupid song," I muttered as a snippet of "True Romance" danced unbidden through my brain. Now the familiar lyrics seemed to taunt me, remind me of everything I couldn't have.

I wandered into the living room, flopping down on the couch without bothering to turn on the lights. Staring into space, I wondered if I'd been stupid to ever believe in true romance. Maybe there was no such thing. At least not the version from that song.

And because I'd believed in some hokey version of true romance, Kaz was with Vanessa now. What if they did fall in love tonight? Stranger things had happened. They were probably the two most amazing people in the world—kind, funny, creative, tons of fun to be around. If they became a couple, I'd have to settle for a front-seat view of their happiness.

I played with a loose thread on the couch cover, trying to banish "True Romance" from my head, but it refused to go. Every line seemed to remind me of how badly I'd messed up.

When you know it's right, it's time to declare.
Make it a memory you two will always share. . . .

I'd been waiting for Trevor to make some kind of big declaration of love. While I'd been waiting, Kaz had been the one who'd pretty much come out and told me he wanted to be more than friends. Only I hadn't really been listening.

I knew my dreams of true romance would all come true
someday.
Like dinner and a movie out with my most special bae. . . .

Okay, so Trevor and I had had fun that night at the movies. But how had I missed that I had even more fun every time I hung out with Kaz, no matter what we were doing? And that it had been that way for as long as I'd known him?

And then there was the biggie:

You'll know it's true on a magical night,
Whether sailing at sea or dancing in the moonlight.
That's when you'll share a first kiss if you dare.
Remember it always: true romance is rare.

• • •

Why had I pinned all my hopes on one magical night? That was stupid. Romance wasn't about a single night, moonlit or otherwise. It wasn't even about a special first kiss. No, now I could see it was much bigger than that gooey movie stuff. It was about being comfortable together, being able to count on each other, being happier when you were together than when you were apart. Like friends, but even a tiny bit better than that.

"Like me and Kaz," I whispered.

As the thoughts and memories tumbled through my head, the song's insanely catchy chorus kept dancing along behind all the rest:

True romance. It's the air that we breathe. Just us two
together. Yeah, just you and me.
True romance. It's the air that we breathe. Just us two
together. Yeah, just you and me.
True romance. It's the air that we breathe. Just us two
together. Yeah, just you and me. . . .

"Stop it!" I exclaimed aloud, pressing both hands over my ears.

That didn't help, so I turned on the TV, punching in one of the satellite music channels. As I surfed around, looking for a song that might be catchy enough to overcome the racket in my head, I heard something outside.

Was that the sound of a car stopping in front of the house? I switched the TV off again, listening. It was too early for my family to be back already, wasn't it? Then again, Timothy sometimes got carsick, especially when he was excited. . . .

I dropped the remote and bolted for the stairs, not ready to face my family—or anyone else—just yet. When I was safely in my room, I shut the door and collapsed against it. Whew! With any luck, they wouldn't even notice I was home.

Holding my breath, I listened for the sound of the door opening downstairs. Instead I heard something else from the direction of the front yard.

I blinked, tilting my head and focusing that way. It sounded like someone was out there under my windows. Was that a giggle?

Yes, definitely a giggle. Followed by . . . the soft toot of a trumpet warming up?

Letting out the breath I'd been holding, I headed for the window to see what was going on out there.

Chapter Twenty

It was Kaz. Of course.

When I opened the window, he grinned up at me. "Oh man," he told the people gathered around him. "We're busted."

"I told you to be quieter," Vanessa chided Dave, the talkative percussionist, who was holding an acoustic guitar under his arm.

I leaned out, not sure what to think. "What are you guys doing down there?"

"Serenading you—duh," a guy from the band—a trombone player named Adam—said loudly. He looked spiffy in his fancy clothes. So did all the others. Dave the percussionist. Cody the sax player. Sophie the French horn player. A couple of others I couldn't see clearly in the dark. And of course, Kaz and Vanessa in their Gatsby getups.

"Ready, guys?" Kaz lifted his trumpet to his lips. "One, two, three . . ."

They all started to play. It was a little raggedy and off tempo at first. But after a few bars, I recognized the tune.

I should. It was the one that had been running through my head for the past half hour.

"'True Romance,'" I blurted out in amazement. But Kaz didn't even like that song! Still, there he was, tootling away at the familiar melody.

Okay, this was too weird. I had to figure out what they were up to, what was going on. How had they even known I was here? For all Vanessa could guess from that text I'd sent, I might have run off somewhere with Trevor.

"Be right down!" I called out the window.

I wasn't sure whether they could hear me over their own playing. But it didn't matter. I raced for the stairs.

Moments later I burst out through the front door. They were just wrapping up the first chorus by then. When he saw me, Kaz stopped playing and grinned.

"Hey," he said.

The others trailed off too, though Cody continued with enthusiasm through the end of the next verse until Dave finally stopped him by yanking the saxophone away from his mouth.

But I wasn't paying attention to that. I was watching Kaz and Vanessa as they came toward me.

"Are you okay?" Vanessa asked. "When I got your text, I was kind of worried."

Kaz nodded. "But just then Maya came by talking about how Jon Whatsisface's girlfriend was all freaking out about him blowing her off and leaving town or something."

"And we kind of figured things out from there," Vanessa finished. She grabbed both my hands and squeezed them. "Are you okay, Chloe?"

"I'm fine." I forced a smile. "He's not worth getting upset about. I can see that now."

"Really?" Kaz stepped forward, looking interested. "Because my offer still stands. You know—if you still want to go to the dance with me? I know I'm not any kind of rock god, but . . ."

"I couldn't," I said quickly. "You and Vanessa—"

"Are just friends," Vanessa finished for me with a smile. "We both knew that all along. We just didn't have the heart to tell you."

"Yeah," Dave put in from a few yards away, where the others were all standing around, pretending not to listen. "Plus Kaz was probably hoping you'd get jealous if you saw him with another woman, Chloe."

"Shut up, Dave," Kaz said quickly.

"Even if that other woman was just, you know, Vanessa," Dave continued.

"Shut up, Dave," Vanessa said with a laugh. She turned to me. "Seriously, Chloe. You were obviously feeling so guilty about turning Kaz down, I might have exaggerated things a little. So you wouldn't worry about him and ruin your big date with Trevor."

I stared at her, taking that in. Then I turned to stare at Kaz. What was that expression on his face? I'd only seen it once before. But if he was embarrassed by what Dave had said, did that mean . . . Could it mean it was true?

"Go to the dance with Kaz, Chloe," Vanessa urged, sincerity and hope shining out of her wide blue eyes. "Seriously. I don't mind at all." She giggled. "Actually, I might be kind of mad at you if you *don't* go."

"Chloe and Kaz sittin' in a tree," Cody sang softly.

"Would you guys please shut up?" Kaz said to Cody and Dave, who grinned at each other and high-fived. Then he turned back to me. "So what do you say, Chloe? Want to give this another try?"

I hesitated. Part of me wanted to say yes. A big part. Especially now that I realized I should have said yes from the start.

But I wasn't sure I could do it. How could I face the whole school after making such a fool of myself over Trevor? After practically forcing my two best friends to go out together? After being so generally clueless about anything having to do with romance, true or otherwise?

Kaz watched my face carefully. After a second he held out his hand.

"Or maybe we don't have to go back," he said. "Maybe we could have our own dance right here." He snapped his fingers. "Maestro?"

Sophie started to play "True Romance" again, and after a few notes the others joined in. Kaz smiled at me, his hand still outstretched.

"May I have this dance?" he said.

I laughed. I couldn't help it. He was so sweet, so adorable, so . . . Kaz. What did I care what anyone else thought?

"No, sorry," I said. As his face started to fall, I quickly added, "But I'd be happy to dance with you to a *different* song."

His face cleared instantly. "In that case," he said, snapping his fingers again. "Maestro! Let's have something a little more interesting, shall we?"

Cody stopped playing. "Like what?"

"We could do 'The Stars and Stripes Forever,'" Adam suggested. "We all know that one."

Dave blew a raspberry in his direction, and Vanessa laughed. "How about something a little more romantic?" She lifted her flute to her lips and started to play.

I recognized the song almost immediately. It was a pretty little Strauss waltz we'd performed at the spring concert last year.

The other musicians nodded and joined in. Soon the old-fashioned music was pouring out over the darkened yard.

I could only imagine what the neighbors were thinking. But I didn't really care. I was focused on Kaz smiling at me, holding out his hand.

"Well?" he said. "May I have this dance?"

"Absolutely." I took his hand in mine, he swung me around, and just like that . . . we were dancing.

And this time there was none of the silliness. None of the crazy spastic moves that had earned Kaz his reputation. No significant risk of concussion, even. He just held me in his arms, swirling me gracefully around the front yard.

"Who knew you could actually dance?" I said softly.

He smiled down at me. "There's a lot you don't know about me," he said with a wink.

That was sort of true, and sort of not. I'd thought I'd known absolutely everything there was to know about Kazuo Aratani. We'd been friends since before we could walk, after all.

But maybe he'd kept a few secrets. Like how he really felt about me. Then again maybe it hadn't been such a secret. Maya had seemed to be clued in. So had Vanessa. Even Trevor hadn't exactly died of shock when he'd figured it out. I was going to have to think about what that meant, but not right now. Right now I just wanted to dance.

Anyway, being in Kaz's arms felt nice. Right. Dare I say—meant to be?

But no. I wasn't going to think that way anymore.

When the song ended, Kaz stepped back and bowed. "Thank you, milady," he said with a hint of his usual goofiness.

I laughed. "So, are we going to the dance or what?" I said loudly enough for everyone to hear.

The others cheered, but Kaz just smiled. "Excellent," he said. "But first there's one quick thing I was hoping we could do to seal the deal."

"What?" I asked.

He stepped forward, taking my hands again. Before I quite knew what was happening, his lips were on mine.

I was so surprised, it took me a second to react. But when he started to pull away, I grabbed him and kept him close, kissing him back.

And it was amazing.

Who knows? I thought, vaguely aware Vanessa and the others were cheering somewhere in the background. Maybe true romance is real after all. . . .

TURN THE PAGE FOR MORE FLIRTY FUN.

Chapter One

It started as just another normal Sunday afternoon. I was wiping down tables at College Avenue Eats. That was normal. My family had owned the place for three generations, and I worked there part-time after school and on weekends.

We were between the end of brunch and the start of the dinner rush, so the place was pretty quiet. There were a couple of university students at the little round tables by the big front window, heads bent over their laptops. An old guy at the counter was nursing a cup of coffee and reading the local paper. Still normal.

My best friend, Simone Amrou, was in the corner booth cramming for tomorrow's biology test. *Definitely* normal. "Opposites attract" was a perfectly sound scientific principle (magnetism, anyone?), but even if it wasn't, I would have believed it based on my lifelong friendship with Simone.

Exhibit A? I'd started studying for the test the same day Mr. Ba announced it two weeks earlier. Simone? Not so much.

"Help me, Bailey!" she wailed as I straightened the salt and pepper shakers on the next table. She widened her puppy-dog brown eyes and stared at me soulfully. That generally worked on guys, especially paired with her exotic good looks. On me? Nuh-uh.

"I told you to read the chapters as we went along." I flicked a stray cupcake crumb off a chair with my rag. "Then you wouldn't have to cram at the last minute."

"I know, Miss Logic, I know." Simone sighed, poufing out her already-full lips to blow a strand of wavy dark hair out of her face. "But I was busy with that English paper all last week, and then Matt wanted to hang out at the park yesterday—"

"Bailey!"

This time it was my cousin calling me from behind the counter. Susannah was nineteen, four years older than me, and a sophomore at the university.

"Be right back," I told Simone. When I reached the counter, Susannah was staring at the cash register with a peevish expression on her round, pretty face. "What's wrong?" I asked. "Did Methuselah die again?"

That was what we called the ancient cash register, which had been around since my great-grandparents started the business. My family was nothing if not consistent.

"Not this time, thank goodness." Susannah smiled, making deep dimples appear on both cheeks. "Do you know where your mom put the register tapes? I can't find them, and she just left to pick up your sister at gymnastics. I can call her, but you know she never picks up when she's driving, and—"

"No, it's okay. I'll find them." I hurried through the swinging saloon-style doors leading into the kitchen. My dad and Uncle Rick—Susannah's father—were just coming in from the delivery bay out back, both of them lugging tubs of donut glaze.

"Can you get the door, Bailey?" Dad grunted as he hoisted his tubs onto the big marble-topped island where Mom and Great-Aunt Ellen rolled out the pastry for the bakery business and the bread for the deli stuff.

I kicked the door shut, then grabbed one of the tubs my uncle was juggling and set it on the stainless-steel counter along the wall. "Suz can't find the register tapes," I said. "Has Mom been reorganizing again?"

My dad traded an amused look with Uncle Rick, who was Mom's brother. "Always," Dad said. "Check the blue cabinet. I think she put the office supplies in there this time."

"Thanks." I headed for the supply room. Everyone in the family knew Mom loved to reorganize. The problem was, she usually moved everything around and then forgot to tell anyone else where she put it all.

When I passed through the kitchen again, Dad was stowing

the last of the tubs under the counter, and Uncle Rick was on the phone.

"Three dozen mixed sandwiches for a week from Saturday?" He jotted something on a pad. "Got it. Will that be delivery or pickup?"

"Spring Thing order?" I asked Dad quietly. The Spring Thing was an annual event at the university—three days of fun, special events, and goofiness to celebrate spring before the crunch of finals set in.

"Guess so." He rubbed his bald spot the way he always did when he was distracted. "Can't believe how many orders we've got already. Gonna be a busy weekend."

"That's good, right? The more orders we get, the more money we make."

He grinned and tousled my chin-length brown hair as if I were still eight years old. "That's my girl," he said. "Always the math whiz!"

"Funny." I smacked his hand away with a laugh, then headed out front with the register tape.

Susannah was on a stool behind the deli case, hunched over a thick textbook. The page it was open to had tons of tiny text and no pictures at all.

"Got a test coming up?" I asked.

"Always." Susannah wrinkled her nose and glared at the book. "Tell me again why I decided to major in business administration? This stuff just doesn't make any sense!"

The little brass bell over the door jingled. A man I vaguely recognized as one of the English professors at the university came in.

Susannah watched as the professor paused to scan the specials board. "Is Deena back from break yet?" she asked me. "Looks like I'm about to have a sandwich order. And the evening crowd will start trickling in pretty soon."

"Don't think so, but our dads are both back there." I flipped open Methuselah's case, which gave way with a creak, and quickly changed out the tape. "They can make a sandwich if they have to."

As Susannah greeted the customer, I headed over to see how Simone was doing. She grabbed my arm and dragged me down onto the seat beside her. "You have to help me, Bails!" She sounded desperate. "I'm so going to flunk tomorrow!"

I glanced at the table. Her textbook was covered in Post-it notes, and other random bits of paper were scattered everywhere. "Okay, where are you stuck?"

"Everywhere," she moaned. "Starting with, what's the difference between DNA and RNA again?"

I sighed. Sadly, this too was normal.

"Okay, so they're both nucleic acids, right?" I said.

She looked blank. "Right?"

"Simone! Didn't you do *any* of the reading?" This was bad even for her. Mr. Ba's class was tough, and he didn't tolerate slackers. It was an accelerated class, and he expected his students to be serious about learning. I loved that. It made me feel like I was already in college learning real stuff instead of marking time in high school.

"I *read* it." Simone stuck her lower lip out in that cute little pout that drove boys crazy. "I just didn't *understand* it. We can't all be science geniuses like you, Myers."

The bell jingled again as another customer came in. I glanced over automatically. I didn't recognize him, which definitely *wasn't* normal, since he was a guy about my own age. There was only one high school in our town, and it was small enough for everyone to know everyone else, by face if not necessarily by name.

Simone spotted the new arrival too. "Who's *that*?" she hissed, elbowing me hard in the ribs.

"Ow! I don't know." I rubbed my ribs and sneaked another look at the guy. He was in line behind the professor, checking out the stuff in the bakery display case while he waited. Kind of tall. Dark brown hair that curled at the temples and the back of his neck. A nose that was a little long and slopey in a way that made his whole face more interesting.

"Maybe he goes to that Catholic school out by the mall," Simone whispered. "Oh! Or he could be a senior from out of town who's touring the campus."

"He doesn't look old enough to be a senior." I shot her a sly look. "But it's a good thing if he's from out of town. You're going out with Matt now, remember? And this guy looks like just the type to tempt you—you know, tall, dark, and handsome."

She tore her gaze away from the guy just long enough to raise one perfectly groomed eyebrow at me. "Yeah, he is pretty cute. It's not like *you* to notice that, though, Bails."

"What? I have eyes." I quickly busied myself straightening her mess of papers. "So back to DNA versus RNA . . ."

"That can wait. Come on, let's go say hi." Simone shoved me out of the booth so energetically I almost hit the floor. I recovered with a less-than-graceful lurch and a grab at the nearest table. Tossing a look toward the counter, I was relieved to see that the guy had his back to me.

"Wait," I hissed. "What are you going to say to him?"

Simone ignored me, grabbing my hand and dragging me along. With my free hand, I quickly smoothed down my hair as best I could. How much had Dad messed it up just now?

And more to the point, what difference did it make? As soon as Mr. Tall Dark and Handsome got a look at Simone, he wouldn't spare a glance for my hair if it was on fire. That was life, and I was used to it. Kind of liked it, actually—it saved me from a lot of embarrassment and stress. Because while I had no trouble chatting with other girls or adults, I was notoriously tongue-tied around guys my own age. I just never seemed to know what to say when faced with that Y chromosome. I was pretty sure it was some kind of syndrome. Maybe I could do a study on it after med school.

Simone, however, was not similarly afflicted. "Hi, there!" she said brightly, tapping the guy on the shoulder. "I'm Simone, and this is my friend Bailey. Are you new in town?"

The guy looked startled, but then he smiled. "Is it that obvious?"

Simone let out her giddiest, most charming laugh. "Only because this is, like, the smallest town in the universe. Right, Bails?"

"Uh?" I said. "I mean, yeah. Except for the university. If you include the student body, I mean, it's actually quite . . . But that's not, you know . . ."

Okay, yes, I was floundering. Obviously. Luckily, Simone came to the rescue. "So are you here for a campus tour, or what?" she asked the guy.

"Not exactly." He looked even cuter when he smiled. "My family just moved here. Actually, we're in the middle of moving in right now—that's why my parents sent me out to pick up some food." He gestured vaguely at the deli counter. "Our new kitchen's kind of a mess."

"You came to the right place," Simone told him. "Eats has the best food in town—just ask Bailey. Her family has run it for like the past million years."

"Really? Cool." The guy turned and studied my face. His eyes were very blue. I held my breath. What was I supposed to do now? My mind was a vacuum. Not as in vacuum cleaner. As in the scientific term for a complete absence of matter or substance.

This time it was Susannah who came to my rescue. "Can I help you?" she called out as the professor moved out of the way, clutching a steaming cup of coffee.

"Yeah, thanks." Mr. Blue Eyes stepped forward. "I need to order some sandwiches to go. . . ."

As he started to give his order, I yanked Simone away. "We should get back to studying."

"Are you mental? We can't abandon your hot new friend." She poked me in the side, making me squawk. "Didn't you see how he was looking at you? And he's obviously smart, too. Just your type."

"What? No. What do you—shut up." I frowned at her.

The loud *cha-ching!* of Methuselah's cash drawer distracted me. I glanced over just as Susannah said "Okay, that'll be about five, ten minutes."

"Thanks." The guy barely had time to turn and face us again before Simone reached out and tugged lightly on the sleeve of his T-shirt.

"MIT, huh?" she said. "That just happens to be Bailey's dream school."

I blinked, noticing his shirt for the first time. It was gray with the red MIT logo emblazoned across the chest. How had I missed that? Or wait—had my subconscious mind somehow picked up on it without telling the rest of me? Maybe that explained why my attention was drawn to this guy with the strength of a neodymium magnet.

"Yeah, both my parents went there," the guy said. "By the way, I'm Logan. Logan Morse."

"Like Morse code?" I blurted out.

See? Hopeless at talking to guys.

Logan laughed. "No relation, as far as I know."

"So Logan," Simone said. "Why'd your family move here?"

"My mom just landed a tenure-track job at the university. Physics. She's really psyched about it."

"Physics? Your mom's a scientist?" I said, interested enough to forget my discomfort for a second.

"Bailey's a scientist too," Simone piped up. "Our bio teacher says she'll probably win the Nobel Prize someday."

I shot her a murderous look. Mr. Ba *so* hadn't said that.

"Really? Cool." Logan gave me another of those appraising blue-eyed looks.

"Um . . ." As I was figuring out whether it was actually scientifically possible to die of embarrassment, three or four people burst into Eats, laughing and talking loudly. College rugby players, I guessed, based on their clothes and the mud covering every inch of them from hair to cleats. Eats was a favorite stop after sports practices thanks to our Belly Buster specials.

"Suz!" one of the rugby players shouted. "Feed us, woman!"

Susannah rolled her eyes and smiled at the player and his friends, then glanced at me. "Think I'm going to need a little help back here, Bailey," she said.

"I've got it!" Simone exclaimed before I could answer. "I'll go make sandwiches. You stay right here, Bails."

I opened my mouth to protest, but it was too late. She was already scooting behind the counter. Simone worked at Eats part-time in the summer, so Susannah just nodded as she pushed past, heading for the kitchen.

As the rugby players clustered around the register, Logan and I stepped back. "This seems like a cool place," he said. "So your family has owned it for a long time, huh?"

"Ages. Since before my mom was born, actually." I was glad he seemed to be ignoring Simone's ridiculous Nobel Prize comment. Still, I couldn't resist turning the topic back to science. "So your mom's a physics prof? And she went to MIT?"

"Yeah. She and Dad met there as undergrads. He's a science guy too—paleontology. He's been working on a book while Mom climbs her way up the academic ranks."

"Works her way up?" I was distracted by the way his lips went a little bit crooked when he smiled, though I wasn't sure why. I didn't usually notice stuff like that about random strangers unless I was doing research for a human-genetics project or something.

"Yeah," he said. "First she was finishing up her PhD; then she had a bunch of nontenured jobs and stuff. So we've lived in a bunch of different places."

"Really? Like where?"

Logan leaned against an empty table. "We just moved here from Switzerland. Before that was Boston—we were only there for a year—and then Tokyo and California. We also spent a couple of summers in Botswana for Dad's research. And one in Singapore for Mom's."

"Wow." I wondered what it would be like to live that way—moving to a new city or country every couple of years.

"So what about you?" Logan asked. "Have you always lived here?"

"Uh-huh." I shrugged. "Totally boring, right?"

"Oh, I don't know." He flashed me that off-kilter smile. "There's something kind of nice about knowing where you belong. Maybe I'll finally find out what that's like. It looks like this time my family might actually stay put for a while."

"Oh." I'd observed Simone talking to guys for long enough to know that she'd probably have a flirty comeback for a comment like that. Me? Not so much. For a moment I'd almost forgotten I was talking to a guy. Now it all came crashing back, and Logan and I stood there staring at each other for what felt like forever but was probably only a few seconds.

"So," he said at last, "what's the local high school like? I'm starting there tomorrow, and I could use any tips you can give me."

"It's okay, I guess." I tried to think of something witty to say but came up empty. "Um, just a typical high school."

The door flew open again. This time at least half a dozen more rugby players poured in. At the same time, Susannah hit the little silver bell by the register.

"Morse!" she called out. "Order's up!"

"That's me." Logan glanced over. "I should get going, I guess. Looks like things are getting busy."

"Yeah. They probably need me to help back there." I stepped aside as a rugby player barreled past, shouting something about a bacon craving.

"Okay." Logan hesitated, shooting another look in Susannah's direction, then turning back to me. "I'll see you at school tomorrow, right, Bailey? You and—um, your friend."

I blinked. Had my ears deceived me, or had this cute guy actually remembered my name—and forgotten Simone's? That had never happened before.

"Yeah," I said just as Susannah shouted my name, sounding frazzled.

"Guess you'd better go. See you." With one last smile, Logan eased his way through the shifting mass of rugby players to grab the big white bag with his name scrawled on it. I noticed there was a smiley face drawn in the *O*—Simone's work, obviously.

Seconds later he was on his way out. I watched him go, feeling oddly disappointed. I figured it was probably because I hadn't learned more about his mother. It was always cool to hear about successful women in science. It gave me hope that my dreams of becoming a biomedical researcher someday could actually come true.

Simone made a beeline for me when I entered the kitchen. "Well?" she demanded. "Tell me everything!"

"Everything?" I grabbed an apron from the hook by the door and tied it around my waist. "That'll take a while."

"Ha-ha, very funny. You know what I mean." She jabbed

me in the arm with a latex-gloved finger. "Logan. You. What happened after I left? Did he ask you out?"

"What? No!" I shot a look at my dad and Uncle Rick to make sure they hadn't overheard. "Are you crazy?"

"Girls!" Uncle Rick's voice rang out from the other end of the huge stainless-steel table, where he was rapidly assembling a pair of roast-beef subs. "More work, less gossip, please."

"*You're* crazy if you missed the way Logan was checking you out," Simone hissed.

There was no more time for talking. Which was just as well, since I had no idea what to say to *that*.